CAUGHT OUT THERE:

A BLACK
PLATONIC-COMEDY
SCREENPLAY

CAUGHT OUT THERE:

A Black Platonic-Comedy Screenplay

by

Tahira Chloe Mahdi
&
Christopher A. Brown

three
zero
media

Published by ThreeZeroMedia

threezeromedia.com

Tuff Crowd Conglomerate is an imprint of ThreeZeroMedia.

Text Design by: ThreeZeroMedia

Cover Design by: ThreeZeroMedia

ISBN: 978-0-9740591-5-0

Distributed by Lightning Source LLC
ingramcontent.com
Printed and bound via IngramSpark in the United States of America

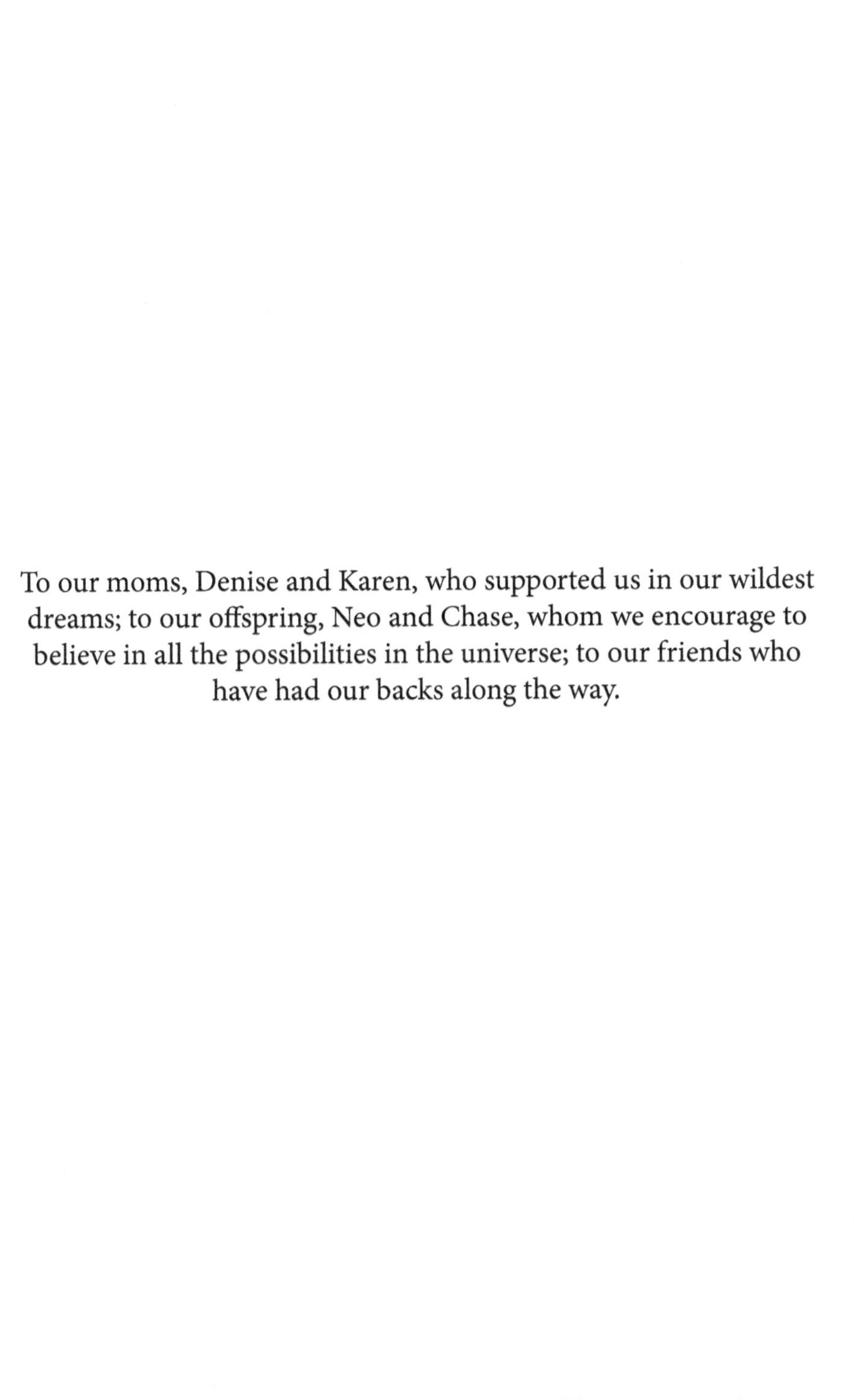

To our moms, Denise and Karen, who supported us in our wildest dreams; to our offspring, Neo and Chase, whom we encourage to believe in all the possibilities in the universe; to our friends who have had our backs along the way.

OPENING IMAGES -

A Newspaper headline fades into view:

Extraterrestrial Emergence Only Exposes Exasperated Earthlings

A second headline replaces the first:

Interplanetary Incomers Ignored Amid Everyday Agitation

A third headline appears:

"F*ck Dem Aliens." Student Loans, Housing, and Food Prices Still Dominate Concerns

CUT TO:

A SEARCH BAR WITH A BLINKING, READY CURSOR

Slowly typed text begins to populate the search bar:

#BLACKALIENS

Followed by a click/enter sound. The screen populates with the following results:

THE VOCAB: Notofearth (not*uhv*urth) - noun

1) Preferred identification of beings from worlds, planets, or societies other than Earth.

2) Adopted nomenclature for extraterrestrial human-form beings arriving on Earth after the year 2020.

3) Black-presenting extraterrestrials.

TRENDING:

The word appears as the screen scrolls downward to reveal more information. A series of social media posts appears under the heading.

@WhiskeysSister: Is it me or are all the Notofearths Black?

@UrUncleRon: If they not from Earth, are they really Black tho?

@THDKR: Not-of-earth Negroes?

@ChadBreezy: So ALIENS can come to the cookout but we can't? Racist.

@MosTheft: I am in negotiations with the aliens. Donate to my new organization and I'll give it to them.

@LikeAHeart: Please take me with yall. I hate it hear. I can spell #Notofearth

The final entry is an article headline from *ThinkPiece Magazine*:

An Alien African Diaspora or Are These Incomers All-The-Way Otherworldly?

Another click sound.

INT. BAR - NIGHT

A man looks up from his phone. We see he is sitting alone
at a bar.

Two **MALE PATRONS** are sitting together near him at the
bar. One checks his watch.

MALE PATRON 1

Aye man, I gotta go in like, 15 minutes.
I told the kids I was goin' to the gym.

His companion motions to the bartender to bring two more
drinks.

Two barstools away, two **FEMALE PATRONS** are having a
heated discussion. One is clearly upset.

FEMALE PATRON 1

...and they gon' let her do MY project!
I'M the one who brought it up at the staff meeting!

Her companion motions to the bartender to bring two more
drinks.

Two barstools away, a woman sits alone. She makes eye
contact with a man sitting at the other end of the bar. They
connect and smile at each other. With her head and eyes,
she asks if the guy wants a drink. The guy indicates yes,
smiles flirtatiously, then gets up and joins her. She motions
to the bartender for two drinks.

A woman (Black, early 30s, curvy) enters the bar, passing
the sign displaying the Thursday night Happy Hour Specials.
This is **HEARTLY**. She sits on a barstool and squints at a
list of drink specials. She nervously glances around, then
pulls out reading glasses. When she looks up, she realizes

the **BARTENDER** is looking directly at her.

HEARTLY
(snatches off her glasses)
Can you recommend something good?

BARTENDER
You cryin', sighin', or celebratin'?

HEARTLY
All o'that.
There's a man I need to forget. Or kill.

BARTENDER
Oh shit. Aight. I got'chu.

A man (Black, early 30s) enters the bar. This is **MALIK**.
He sits two seats down from Heartly.

BARTENDER
What up main man?

MALIK
What up. Gimme a Revolver, man.

BARTENDER
Oh shit. You too?

MALIK
Damn.
You got somebody else up for the six-shooter?

The Bartender nods toward Heartly.

HEARTLY
(looking from the bartender to Malik)
Hold up... what'chu 'bout to give me?

The Bartender sets up six shot glasses in front of Malik and six in front of Heartly. He pours different liquids into a cocktail shaker.

HEARTLY
Wait... can I get something a little more... feminine?

BARTENDER
You said you wanna forget the dude or kill him.
That's what the Revolver is for.

HEARTLY
(takes a deep breath)
Okay.

She looks at Malik.

MALIK
We in the same boat, I see.

HEARTLY
Bad breakup?

MALIK
If we was even IN a damn relationship... *(thinks)* Nah, I KNOW we were! Damn Leos, man. And I ain't even into that birthday Zodiac shit, but my boys warned me about them damn Leos!

Heartly gasps and moves to the seat next to Malik. The bartender fills their shot glasses.

HEARTLY
NOOOO! Oh my gosh!
I'M about to kill a Leo!! What'd yours do?

They both take a shot.

MALIK

So... she's a party promoter. 'Round-the-town socialite, social media model, *(does finger quotes)* influencer, the whole nine...

CUT TO:

FLASHBACK:

INT. NIGHTCLUB - NIGHT

Malik follows behind **RHONDA** (late 20s, Instagram model-type, ambiguous race) who seems to know EVERYONE as she passes by them. A lively hip hop groove plays as enthusiastic clubgoers dance and socialize.

Malik watches her hug and kiss every guy she passes and speak to each of them by name. As she progresses through the club, each interaction seems to get more personal and intimate. Finally they reach the **OWNER** (Black man, tall, 40s) of the club.

RHONDA

HAYYYYYY BOO! You been workin' out? You lookin' extra fine...

OWNER

A little bit. Good to see you, Rhonda. You gon' have to let me take you out again. Last time was... memorable.

MALIK

AHEM.

Rhonda ignores Malik as she leans in to the owner and whispers something in his ear. The Owner laughs and hugs her, sneakily slipping a hand over her rear. Malik sees the movement and steps forward but Rhonda laughs, runs her hand across the owner's chest while moving the other hand off of her posterior, and walks away.

Malik stares the owner down before Rhonda grabs him by the hand and drags him away. Malik starts to push her away when someone hands Rhonda a mic. She addresses the crowd.

RHONDA

Hey ya'll! Thanks for coming out tonight! We gon' get this party started! Where my Notofearths at?

CUT TO:

EXT. NIGHTCLUB - LATER

Rhonda steps out of the club. Malik follows a few steps behind, furious. They walk a few steps before he finally speaks.

MALIK

What the hell was that?

RHONDA

A party?

MALIK

You know what I'm talking about. How many times we gonna do this? Every dude, every club. Like you know every dude in the club intimately!

RHONDA

And?

MALIK

You have a man. This is mad disrespectful. And that shit with the owner? What the --

RHONDA
THIS is why I'm the best promoter in the city.
Everybody knows me,
and I make EVERYBODY feel special.

Rhonda notices that bystanders have gathered. She reaches into her bra and holds up a wad of cash.

RHONDA (cont'd)
This money ain't disrespectful.
And right now I'm about this money. Can I live?

MALIK
What about us?

A few bystanders have pulled out their phones and started streaming in hopes that something ridiculous will jump off. Rhonda takes advantage of the situation.

RHONDA
@RhondaBooBaby is an independent woman!
She don't need nobody but her 124,333 follow--

Her phone dings. Another follower!

RHONDA
Oop! 124,334 followers.
You can either get on the train or you can step.

Malik takes a step back and looks at the cameras recording.

CUT TO:

INT. BAR - PRESENT

Malik shakes his head as Heartly holds up her phone. A YouTube video is already set up titled "@RhondaBooBaby

Disses Random Dude."

HEARTLY
Oh shit! This was you?!
I follow RhondaBooBaby!
I'll be honest, I laughed my ass off at this,
but I felt bad for you. Dang!

Malik holds up another shot, she takes hers, and they clink
glasses. They drink.

MALIK
Your turn.

HEARTLY
Well... speaking of videos... Here is the Leo I want to kill.

Heartly types on her phone then hands it to him. A video by
**THE HONORABLE DR. KIMET ROBINSON
(THDKR)** is playing. We can tell that he is at a desk in a
hotel room, talking into his laptop camera. He is being serious but looks ridiculous because he is wearing a PaRappa
the Rapper hat.

VIDEO:

THDKR
I see all these queens doin' sit-ups, usin' all these exercises
and devices tryna get a small waistline. You are not meant to
have a small waist, sisters! Your waist is meant to expand, so
that YOU can carry the next generation of warriors! That's
why we call you WOMB-MAN. Your womb is your connection to the divine. You need that extra flesh around your
waist to protect the life inside...

Malik snickers as he stops the video and hands the phone
back to Heartly.

MALIK
I can't... I can't...
(downs a shot)
And you fell for that hotep shit?

HEARTLY
You know, your use of the term "hotep" is not...

MALIK
(cutting her off)
Daaammmnnn! You had a Leo hotep!

Heartly opens her mouth to argue, but Malik cuts her off again.

MALIK
You had a Leotep!

Heartly looks at Malik as if she is going to cut him, but he can't stop laughing.

MALIK
I'm sorry, I'm sorry. Go ahead.

HEARTLY
I fell for a man that I trusted to love me for who I am! Didn't have to work out, didn't have to shave, didn't have to wear makeup...

She downs a shot.

MALIK
Or weren't allowed to...

She missed his remark, and is staring off in another direction.

HEARTLY
I could be just ME. And somebody loved it.

MALIK
So, what happened?

HEARTLY
(takes a deep breath)
I came home one day...

MALIK
(cutting her off)
You let him move in, didn't you?

HEARTLY
He was between places... All he had was a suitcase and a
laptop. Shut up. Anyway...

FADE TO:

FLASHBACK:

INT. HEARTLY'S LIVING ROOM - EVENING
Cut to an apartment living room, decorated with an overly
exaggerated "African" theme. This is Heartly's apartment.
Jazz music is playing. Heartly walks in her front door, just
coming home from work. THDKR is standing in the middle
of the room. He is wearing a washed out undershirt and
basketball shorts.

HEARTLY
Guess who broke out early?

THDKR
(nodding slowly)
In divine time, there is no early, no late. Everything happens
when it should.

HEARTLY
You on it already, huh?
(sniffs the air)
And you're cooking too?

THDKR
Have a seat.

Heartly plops down on the sofa and puts her feet up.
THDKR is still standing. Heartly is looking at him as if she
expects him to bring her a plate of the food she smells.

THDKR
As my first wife...

HEARTLY
(happily)
Yes, your wi... Hol' up. First?

THDKR
(calmly cuts her off)
You know I'm building my village.
You will always be the first queen.
And YOU will get to approve any others.

HEARTLY
Others?

THDKR
(calls to the closet)
Queen... come on out, queen.

The closet door bangs and won't open. Someone inside
can't get out. Heartly jumps up.

CLOSET GIRL
(quietly)
Help?

THDKR shakes his head and goes over to open the closet door. **CLOSET GIRL** (Black, 20s, barely over 5 feet tall) hesitates to come out. THDKR walks over to her and gently pulls her out of the closet.

She is wearing a t-shirt that reads "Hon. Dr. Kimet Robinson 2015 Tour" with a picture of his face.

Heartly is still standing, stunned, with her mouth open. This is the first time we can see that Heartly is taller than THDKR. But the woman is shorter than THDKR.

THDKR
My other queens will be able to look UP to me, and...

HEARTLY
WHAT?!

THDKR
And, like her, they should be half my age,
plus seven, so...

HEARTLY
She can't even find her way out a closet!
What kind of bullshi--

Heartly's rant of obscenities is heard as a series of bleeps. The scene cuts abruptly.

CUT TO:

INT. BAR - PRESENT

Heartly downs another shot. Malik does the same.

MALIK
Ouch. And now you gotta go through a divorce?

HEARTLY
Hell no, we weren't married for real!
Thank God...
He ain't a real doctor either.
It's like a community-earned title that...

Heartly realizes how ridiculous it all sounds and then takes another shot. Malik follows suit.

MALIK
So what's your name, sweetheart?

HEARTLY
(*with attitude*)
Sweetheart?

MALIK
(*mockingly*)
Queeeen?

Heartly is not amused.

MALIK
Nice to meet you. I'm Malik.

He offers his hand, but Heartly acts disgusted.

HEARTLY
Malik? Unh uh.
That's too much Kwanzaa.
Is that your real name?
I don't wanna meet no Malik,
no Ra-sheed, no Wah-seem...

MALIK
Well forget you too.
Fake doctor got you hatin' on REAL names?

Heartly takes the fifth shot. She appears to be disgusted with herself. She turns to Malik and offers her hand.

HEARTLY
I'm Heartly.

MALIK
Like the motorcycle?

HEARTLY
No, like a heart. Heart-ly.

MALIK
(flinching)
Yeah, after a Rhonda-Boo-Baby,
I damn sure don't wanna meet no Heart-lee.

Heartly is about to respond when the bartender returns.

BARTENDER
Alright. So, before you take your last shots,
I offer you a menu to feed all o'dat...
(hands Heartly a menu)
AND a list of our recommended rideshare drivers.
(hands Malik a laminated list)
I'll give y'all a minute.
(walks away)

As Malik and Heartly glance over the menu and the list, the music changes to something more upbeat. They look over their shoulders and see that a DJ is spinning vinyl. We hear Billy Ocean's "NIGHTS (FEEL LIKE GETTIN' DOWN)" and see that they're both drunk.

HEARTLY
I love this song! When did a DJ set up?

MALIK
Oh HELL YES.

They both yell for the bartender and we see a montage of them taking selfies, dancing, and clinking beers and glasses of water, eating wings, and feeding each other fries.

CUT TO:

INT. RIDESHARE CAR - NIGHT

The **RIDESHARE DRIVER** shakes her head and looks at Heartly and Malik in the rearview mirror. They are clearly drunk.

RIDESHARE DRIVER
How ya'll doin'?

HEARTLY
(slurred)
As long as you ain't a Leo, we all good!
Wait, when's your birthday?

RIDESHARE DRIVER
July 11th.

MALIK
Oh Halleluyer!

The driver shakes her head and turns the radio up just a little. A woman is singing a cover of the Caught Out There original song "OVER YOU" by Kato Hammond and Tahira Mahdi.

HEARTLY
Turn it up, DJ!

As the music turns up, Heartly and Malik look at each other in anticipation of the hook. Then, they start to sing loudly.

HEARTLY AND MALIK
AND I'M OVER YOU!
YOU DON'T OWN MY MIND!
AND I'M SOBER NOW!
AND YOU AIN'T THAT FINE!
AND I'M OVER YOU!
AND I HATE YOU TOO!
AND I'M BETTER NOW!
AND I'M THROUGH WITH YOU!

CUT TO:

INT. MALIK'S APARTMENT - NIGHT

Heartly is on his couch, grabbing a pillow to settle in for the night. Malik tosses her a blanket. She snuggles into it.

MALIK
You need an alarm?
You goin' to work tomorrow?

Heartly snores loudly. Malik goes to his room and closes the door.

FADE TO BLACK.

INT. MALIK'S APARTMENT - MORNING

Heartly's cell phone alarm is going off. She wakes up and realizes she is not in her own place. She slowly sits up and her hair is all messed up. Her eye makeup is smeared.

MALIK
Mornin' sunshine.

Heartly is startled, then embarrassed. She looks down and is still fully dressed.

Malik is sitting at his dining room table, typing on his laptop. He appears to be wide awake and unaffected by the previous night's drinking.

Heartly groans and shoots him an evil look.

He laughs as he gets up and goes to the fridge. He takes out a Gatorade, and brings it to her.

She takes it and groans again. He gently fluffs the pillow behind her in order to prop her up. He takes the Gatorade, opens it for her, and hands it back to her. She takes a drink.

MALIK
You goin' to work today?

HEARTLY
(groans and mutters unintelligibly)

Malik walks back to his laptop.

MALIK
No worries. You can chill for a while. I work from home.

Heartly slowly sits up and puts her feet on the floor.

HEARTLY
Bathroom?

Malik points in the direction of the bathroom. Heartly stands up and walks slowly to the bathroom.

CUT TO:

As she sits on the toilet, she notices that the bathroom is decorated with a Black superhero theme. She half-smiles in approval.

CUT TO:

Heartly looks in the mirror as we hear the end of the flush of the toilet. She jumps back when she sees her reflection. Her hair is a mess and her mascara is smudged all around her eyes.

She turns on the faucet and washes her hands quickly. She starts wadding toilet paper to use to wipe off her eye makeup.

CUT TO:

Malik continues to work on his laptop.

CUT TO:

Heartly opens his medicine cabinet. She also peeks behind his shower curtain. She looks back at the sink and notices two toothbrushes in a holder. She looks at the towel rack and sees two used full-sized towels that are different colors, indicating that they have been used by two different people.

HEARTLY
Roommate. Mmph.

She walks back to the living room and grabs the Gatorade.

MALIK
Hungry?

HEARTLY
(thinks for a second)
Uh...

MALIK
I'm just bein' hospitable.

He gets up and goes to the fridge.

MALIK (cont'd)
You DID just wake up on my couch.
I'd offer a stray dog somethin' to eat.

Heartly acts mildly offended at his comment. Malik scans
the contents of his refrigerator.

MALIK
I got...eggs, blueberry muffins,
creamed chipped beef, grapes,
chicken sausage, pork bacon...
(shuts fridge)
Grits, oatmeal...?

HEARTLY
Where's the roommate?

MALIK
My roommate?
(looks as if he wonders what she knows)
He won't be back until tonight.

HEARTLY
You know the last time I had actual, pork bacon?

FADE TO:

Dirty breakfast dishes are on the coffee table. Heartly and

Malik on his couch, full from breakfast, with coffee mugs in their hands. Malik grabs the remote control and turns on the TV.

HEARTLY
Why would you say you had pork bacon
if you weren't willing to cook it?

MALIK
I don't eat that stuff.
That's his, the roommate's. I don't dig the swine.

HEARTLY
Hotep...

MALIK
(laughing)
I'ma wipe that makeup off your face too!
Better not have eff'd up my pillow!

Malik grabs for the pillow as Heartly swats his hand away playfully and laughs.

HEARTLY
Stop! I'm too full to fight you.

She turns her attention to the TV and starts to laugh.

HEARTLY
What is this?

MALIK
Public access channel.
I support the LOCALS.

A commercial comes on. It's a cheesy, low-budget commercial advertising a local astrologer who can act as a match-

21

maker for singles, based on their zodiac signs.

The commercial begins with Kato & the Allykats'
"ZODIAC," a go-go version of the familiar refrain "What's
that number one zodiac sign?" from Uncle Luke's "It's Your
Birthday" as neon-colored zodiac symbols swirl around the
screen.

MALIK
SCORPIO!!

HEARTLY
Ew.

When the line comes again, "I said, what's that number one
zodiac sign?" Heartly yells out.

HEARTLY
Gem-in-iiiiiii!!

MALIK
Ugh.

The commercial goes from ratchet to faux-ethereal in a
matter of seconds. Couples of all types give testimonies on
how it worked for them.

MAN FROM COUPLE 1
I knew I needed the gentleness of a Cancer woman,
and Miss Niecey hooked it up.

WOMAN FROM COUPLE 1
(looks bored)
I mean... he'll do...

CUT TO:

WOMAN FROM COUPLE 2
I wanted a Taurus. They take care of you.

Her female partner turns her head to glare at her.

CUT TO:

A man stares lovingly and longingly at his partner.

WOMAN FROM COUPLE 3
(deadpan)
I didn't expect an Aries to be so... attentive.
But, Miss Niecey knows best.

MAN FROM COUPLE 3
(grabs his partners hand)
You hungry babe?

VOICEOVER
Your love is out there.
Let the stars be your guide.
Call and let Miss Niecey hook you up today!

Malik and Heartly are cracking up laughing. Heartly uses her phone to take a picture of the screen.

HEARTLY
(sarcastically)
You support local shit, huh?
Is this how you get dates?

MALIK
Not yet, but shoot, I'd try it.

HEARTLY
No you wouldn't!

MALIK
Yes, I would.
Shoot, I'd do it just to write about it.

HEARTLY
You're a writer?

MALIK
That's... one of the things I do.

Heartly is trying not to be impressed.

HEARTLY
Hmm. You should do it.

MALIK
What do you do for work?

HEARTLY
Good ol' city gub'ment.

MALIK
Ahh. I never woulda guessed.

HEARTLY
So, are you gonna do it?

MALIK
Why you tryna get me to do this?

HEARTLY
I can't just look at a commercial like that and let it go!
I need SOMEBODY I know to do it!

MALIK
So, do it yourself!

HEARTLY
No! I am NOT that desperate!

MALIK
(offended)
But I am?

Heartly realizes her mistake and softens a bit.

HEARTLY
No... not like...

MALIK
'Cause YOUR love life is going soooo well...

HEARTLY
OK, we'll both do it.
It'll be the best way for us to move on.
Just get some rebound dates in our systems,
have some fun, and... move on.

MALIK
You're getting into it, aren't you?

HEARTLY
Come on, Scorpio!
Y'all supposed to be the freaks of the industry!
Is there a law that says we have to sit at home
crying about our breakups? We can't date and move on?

Malik nods in agreement. This makes sense.

MALIK
I like your logic, lady.

Heartly raises her coffee mug.

HEARTLY
To moving on, having fun, no tears!

MALIK
To moving on, having fun, no tears.

They clink mugs. Heartly smirks as she picks up her phone and dials.

FADE TO:

EXT. SENIOR LIVING FACILITY - DAY

Malik is sitting on a bench outside the building. He's on his phone going through a social media feed. He sees a pic of him and Heartly from the other night.

He clicks to see more of her pics and sees several of her in costumes. It appears she is into cosplay. Each costume is more elaborate than the last, and she's actually really good at it.

MALIK
(Out loud to himself, in disbelief)
No. Mickey-fickey. Way.

He clicks off the screen and puts his phone away, obviously amused at Heartly's cosplay life.

A man, well-dressed, in his 30s, walks up. Malik looks up at him for a beat before the man sits down.
This is **MICHAEL**, Malik's brother.

MICHAEL
You coulda just gone in.

MALIK
(shakes his head and sighs)
I don't like nursing homes.
Especially since Pop lives in one now.

MICHAEL
They don't even call this a nursing home. It's assisted living.
He's doing good. You worry too much.

MALIK
And he don't even hate us.

MICHAEL
He's a reasonable man. Always has been.
(stands up)
Come on.

Malik stands up and they both walk toward the front door
of the upscale senior facility.

CUT TO:

INT. POPS' SMALL APARTMENT - MOMENTS LATER

Malik and Michael are sitting in arm chairs. A nurse has just
finished adjusting Pops' nasal cannula for an oxygen tank.
She pats him on the shoulder, smiles at Malik and Michael,
and leaves. Pops watches the nurse walk away with interest.

POPS
Don't come see me with no sad faces.
Y'all better talk about women or something.

MICHAEL
Too soon, Pops. You know "Master Malik" here is having
woman problems.

He chuckles at Malik, who gives him the side eye of death.

POPS
Sheeeeit. He just got rid of the problem.
Never trust a woman with titties that big
and a waist that small.
(with naughty interest)
Were they real?

MALIK
Can we PLEASE talk about something else?

POPS
Other than titties?
I may not be long for this world! Tell me 'bout some titties!

Pops and Michael laugh. Their favorite pastime is
annoying Malik, who never fails to amuse them with his
irritated reactions.

POPS
Ok. Fine, we'll talk about the next best thing. Money.

MICHAEL
Next best?

POPS
Shut up. We almost got him smilin' now.

MALIK
We got the paperwork squared away.
Looks like we're good with the will, the accounts, and
everything we need. Your financial planner is a beast.

POPS
Ain't she though?
Smarter than my TWO computer genius sons. Y'all gotta

promise me you'll get yourselves smart women.

MICHAEL
Here we go...

POPS
I mean it, though. That's a lot of money you're coming into.
Get a smart woman... or... whatever you gonna get... I'm too
old to judge... I love you either way.

Malik and Michael look at each other and then laugh.

MICHAEL
Now that we got you settled in here, I was thinking...
I can move here and set up shop. I can buy a place nearby.
I got products to sell and places to sell it.

POPS
Son, do whatever's gonna make you happy. Both of you, I
want you to be happy. I know you probably gettin' on your
brother's damn nerves stayin' wit' him.
(laughs)

MICHAEL
I ain't thinkin' 'bout him.

MALIK
He still eatin' that pork bacon.

POPS
I knew it.

FADE TO:

EXT. TEA AND SAMMICHES CAFE - DAY
Heartly is standing outside on a city street with her cell

phone to her ear. We hear Malik's voice say, "It's Malik. Leave a message."

HEARTLY
I was going to text, but I want you to hear my voice for this reminder of our appointment this evening.
Don't you dare back out or I will never speak to you again!
Wait, you'd probably like that, so...
(eye roll)
Anyway, we made a pact! Also, dinner!
Before! Or after. Whatever.

Heartly hangs up and puts the phone away as a woman (Black, 30s, professional) walks up behind her. This is Heartly's cousin **STACEY**.

STACEY
Cuz!

Heartly turns toward Stacey, startled.

STACEY
You good?

HEARTLY
Yes! Just taking care of some business.

CUT TO:

INT. TEA AND SAMMICHES CAFE - DAY

Heartly and Stacey walk into a small café that sells tea, sandwiches, soup, smoothies, and coffee. A bell on the door signals their entrance and a young man behind the counter sees them, smiles, and comes from behind the counter. This is **JONATHAN** (early 20s, fun and bubbly).

He is Heartly's biggest fan and she knows it, and he knows that she knows it. They have an understanding of empty flirtation. He goes over to a table by the window and takes off a "Reserved" sign.

JONATHAN
What's up, Miss Heartly, Miss Stacey.
I got'chall right here.

HEARTLY
Thank you, Jonathan.

STACEY
Hi, Jonathan. I'll have the usual, thanks.

HEARTLY
I need a menu, please.

JONATHAN
My woman is fickle, I love it!

He takes a menu off another table and places it in front of Heartly.

JONATHAN
Holla back when you decide.
In the meantime, check out the tunes!
(points to an overhead speaker)
It's my new album.

STACEY
Oh, check you out!

HEARTLY
(subdued, distracted)
That's so cool, Jonathan. Congratulations.

Jonathan heads back to the counter. Instead of reading the menu, Heartly absently stares out of the window. Stacey glares at her for two seconds before getting her attention.

STACEY
One more time. Are. You. Ok?

HEARTLY
I can't even concentrate at work anymore. My mind is just filled with designs and plans and... visions.

STACEY
Well, good! We'll give it another year, and get started on your grand business plan.

HEARTLY
Another year? Stacey, this is NOW!
I'm already started. Look...

She pulls an organized three-ring binder from her bag and hands it to Stacey.

HEARTLY
I even added earrings! Can you picture it?
Blouses AND earrings?

STACEY
(looking through it, nodding)
This is good stuff.
Great, now I'm under pressure and I can't keep up.

HEARTLY
It's not about keeping up; it's about a partnership!
Our family business, Cousins In Cahoots?
We talked about this at length!

STACEY
Girl, I was drunk!

HEARTLY
I was serious, though!
Are you saying you were just playin'?

Jonathan returns to the table.

JONATHAN
You decide, Miss Heartly?

HEARTLY
(sadly)
I'm not hungry anymore.
(hands him the menu)
Thanks.

JONATHAN
(concerned as he takes the menu)
Alright. I got somethin' for you. Hold tight.

Jonathan rushes off.

STACEY
I was serious. But I was also dreaming.
It's starting a WHOLE business.

HEARTLY
Our designs are good! We can't start off expecting to fail!

STACEY
I JUST got married. I JUST had a baby.

HEARTLY
And?

STACEY
Can you imagine me trying to explain some crazy business
scheme to Chris? My money isn't just MINE anymore!

HEARTLY
Oh, now it's a crazy business scheme?

STACEY
(sucks teeth)
Oh, not like that. But I'm not an "I" anymore; I'm a "we."

Jonathan sets down a plate with a panini and an iced tea in
front of Stacey. He sets down a green smoothie in front of
Heartly.

JONATHAN
That's my special Stress Relief smoothie. On the house.
Let me know what you think.

Heartly looks up at him and smiles gratefully. He gives her a
nod and walks away.

Heartly reaches out for her notebook and Stacey hands it
back. Heartly puts it in her bag.

STACEY
I believe in you. And I will ALWAYS be here to cheer you on,
to listen to you, all that. But, I'm not ready to invest time
and money into a company right now.
That's as honest as I can be about it.

HEARTLY
(nods slowly)
Thank you for your honesty.

STACEY
But, back to you.

Girl, you are my latest, greatest inspiration. I admire you. Not just your hustle, but your bravery. Your faith.

Heartly smiles weakly.

HEARTLY
(short sigh)
I'll keep you posted, then.

Right beside their table, a **Notofearth** materializes out of thin air with an audible POP sound, alarming Stacey and Heartly.

STACEY
(angrily)
EXCUSE ME! Can you watch where you pop in?!

NOTOFEARTH PATRON
Aw, my bad, sis. I'm just meetin' my crew.

The Notofearth waves to a group of people on the other side of the room and walks toward them.

STACEY
(scoffs)
"Sis"? They doin' THAT now?

HEARTLY
Don't be like that. They Black too.

STACEY
(with attitude)
What Black people you know can pop in and out like that?

HEARTLY
Them!

STACEY
Unh-unh. Can't trust it. Not til we know who's who and
what's what... Girl, drink your drink.
(muttering and picking up her panini)
...this weird shit...

INT. HEARTLY'S CAR - NIGHT

Malik is getting into the passenger seat of Heartly's car.
She smiles as if she is taunting him.

HEARTLY
Well, at least you smell good.

MALIK
It's not the incense you used to, but I do aight.

HEARTLY
Ha.

She drives off.

HEARTLY
Your social media is skimpy, dude.
I tried to search for some dirt and got nothing.
You even get shadowed out in that video when homegirl
dumped you in the street.

MALIK
Is THAT what you want for my life?
My dirt out in the street?

HEARTLY
Yeah, like the rest of us!

MALIK
You got me right here.
Anything you want to know, just ask.

HEARTLY
(side-eyes)
Hmph.

Malik continues to look forward, and smiles as if he knows something she doesn't. She makes a turn into a shopping center.

HEARTLY
Why is this place so close by? And in a shopping center?

We see that the shopping center is definitely NOT upscale.

MALIK
You mad it's nearby?

HEARTLY
I was mad when I found out YOU lived so close to me.

MALIK
Right? Might have to see your nosey ass in the grocery
store... All up in my cart and whatnot.

HEARTLY
Any interaction you have with me will improve your life.
You better believe THAT.

Heartly parks in the lot in front of the building.

MALIK
Says the person who just drove me to Miss Niecey's
Astrology Centre to get a date.

HEARTLY
You mean the person helping you
forget all about Big Booty Wanda?

Malik glares at her as he opens the car door.

                                        CUT TO:

INT. MISS NIECEY'S ASTROLOGY CENTRE - MOMENTS
LATER

Heartly and Malik enter the store. A wind chime alerts
anyone inside to their presence. The pair are taken aback
by the décor.

Planets and stars hang from the ceiling like bad science
projects. Posters line the walls charting the paths of the
different signs through their lives. There's also a section
marked love potions, but it is empty.

MALIK
Oh this is completely ridic--

A door opens in the back and a figure emerges. This is
MISS NIECEY (Black, ethereal, ageless, and fabulous).

MISS NIECEY
Malik? Heartly?

HEARTLY
(*suddenly nervous*)
That's us.

MISS NIECEY
Nice to meet you.

Miss Niecey walks to them and shakes their hands.

MISS NIECEY
Have a seat.

Malik and Heartly sit in front of a desk.

The rest of the place looks like a typical magic & potion shop from a movie, but the computer, desk, and tech accessories behind Miss Niecey look like the inside of the 1960s version of the *Star Trek* Enterprise--outdated and amazing.

MISS NIECEY
It says a lot about you two that you wanted to do this together. Very supportive behavior. I'll remember that in both matching processes.

Heartly and Malik look at each other and nod, seeming to agree to keep going with the process.

MALIK
So, what's up first? Questionnaires?

MISS NIECEY
Questionnaires?

MALIK
Yeah, personality tests, or something?

MISS NIECEY
Oh no, we don't match that way.

Miss Niecey hits a button and a screen comes on that is a person sitting, appearing to be being interviewed.

MISS NIECEY
First, I'm going to suggest what I think is a good place to
start for each of you. And then I match you
with someone of my choice.

Heartly and Malik look confused.

MISS NIECEY
You look confused. It's like this.
Heartly, I'm going to start you off with a Libra.
(studying Heartly, nodding slowly)
You could use some understanding
without judgment right now.

Heartly looks impressed and interested. Miss Niecey has
pushed the right buttons.

HEARTLY
Hm. Ok, and what if I don't like the person?

MISS NIECEY
If my first choice doesn't work for you, then I can match you
with another person of the same sign, OR you can request
a different sign. Now, if you'll focus your attention on that
green dot there...

Malik and Heartly's eyes find the green dot in front of them
and a camera flashes.

MISS NIECEY
Thank you.

Malik and Heartly are startled.

MALIK
Damn, you coulda said, "Say cheese!"

HEARTLY
I wasn't ready!

Miss Niecey is punching buttons on the panel, not looking at them.

MISS NIECEY
Stay ready and you ain't gotta get ready.
(turns back to them)
This ain't a modeling agency; we match spirits.
This is small potatoes.

Miss Niecey smiles as if she knows something they don't.

MALIK
(slightly concerned)
Which sign do I get?

MISS NIECEY
(quick head tilt)
You could use a win right now.
A Pisces will make you feel breezy enough
to get your confidence back up.

HEARTLY
You ARE good.

MISS NIECEY
Oh-kayyyy? My success rate is 62%!

MALIK
(skeptical)
Sixty-two?

MISS NIECEY
Significantly more than half.

Malik and Heartly exchange glances. Miss Niecey slaps the table, jerking their attention back to her.

MISS NIECEY
Say it with me. "Miss Niecey is NOT CRAZY."

HEARTLY AND MALIK
Miss Niecey is not crazy.

Miss Niecey smiles and continues.

MISS NIECEY
And if y'all were pulling more than 0%,
you wouldn't be sitting here now, would you?

Heartly and Malik are shocked by the dragging.

MISS NIECEY
Welcome to Miss Niecey's Multiverse-Soul Singles.

As their mouths drop open at the word "multiversal," the camera flashes again, and we get that pic onscreen before it fades to black and white.

CUT TO BLACK.

EXT. DOWNTOWN FRENCH RESTAURANT - EVENING

Heartly walks up the sidewalk to the restaurant's facade, finishing her conversation on the phone.

HEARTLY
...I'm at Lavida's French on Obama Avenue. If you don't hear from me in two hours, send a search team.

Heartly hangs up and walks inside.

INT. DOWNTOWN FRENCH RESTAURANT - EVENING

The restaurant is empty. She starts to back away when her date **DEVIN** (a good-looking Black man) comes from the back.

DEVIN
Heartly? It's me, Devin. Welcome, have a seat.

HEARTLY
Umm... you know this is suspect as hell, right? And I did let several people know where I am, so don't...

DEVIN
Calm down, calm down. I know the owner. This place is ours for as long as we need it.

HEARTLY
What are you, some Godfather type of gangsta?
Makin' people offers they can't refuse?

Wait staff comes from the kitchen, bringing plates of dessert. One of them is holding two menus and pulls out a chair.

WAITER
Welcome, Heartly.
Tonight, we start with dessert.

HEARTLY
(walking toward the table)
Is that crème brulee ?

CUT TO:

Heartly is sipping wine while Devin is finishing a story.

DEVIN

So, yeah, he is kind of a godfather to me. And, he's a hopeless romantic, so he was totally down for this.

HEARTLY

Isn't this a bit much for a first date with a stranger?

She takes a bite of her Lobster Thermidor and wrinkles her nose. She's not really a fan.

DEVIN

The service says that Geminis demand romance and that you have high-profile tastes. I figured I could keep up with that. I'm a romantic, myself.

Devin smiles at her confidently.

HEARTLY

Well, you should rethink this kind of thing on a first date. It's creepy as hell.

Devin is taken aback, but attempts to remain in a positive mood.

DEVIN

Just trying to follow directions
and give a lady what she wants.

HEARTLY

Well, you know the owner. It's kind of like... I don't know... cheating. You didn't have to put any real thought into it. It's like, textbook "What to Do to Impress Someone."

DEVIN

Are you serious?

HEARTLY
Yeah, I am. And what's up with this Darius Lovehall vibe
you're giving off? Between the leather jacket and the looks
you're giving me, I feel like you're about to start quoting bad
poetry or something. I bet you got a motorcycle outside too.
Don't you?

Devin looks mildly offended, but then grins confidently.

DEVIN
You're funny. And I see where you're coming from with that,
but I assure you I've got at least one original idea for tonight.
If you're done here, I can show you.

Heartly half smiles and stands. Devin nods to the waitstaff
who open the door for them. As they step outside she sees
a horse drawn carriage parked in front of the restaurant.

DEVIN
Your chariot awaits, my lady.

HEARTLY
Oh. My. Word.

Heartly stares in disbelief for a moment before bursting into
a fit of laughter. She laughs so hard she can barely catch her
breath. Devin's confident smile slowly fades as he turns to
watch her nearly falling over, convulsing in hysterics.

DEVIN
What--

HEARTLY
Oh man. That...that's the corniest shit I've ever seen. Hooom-
mmygawd. I...I can't with this.

Heartly takes her phone out, turns around and takes a selfie.

                                                    CUT TO:

A screenshot of a post to her social media account with the
picture she just took and the caption, "This corny MF right
here!"

                                               CUT BACK TO:

Devin pinches the bridge of his nose and exhales deeply
before addressing Heartly.

DEVIN
OK. That settles that.
We're clearly on VERY different pages. You're obviously
either not ready for someone to try and treat you well, or
you're so miserable that no one will ever make you happy.
Either way, we're done here.

With that, Devin hops on the horse and kicks his heels. The
horse rears up and gallops off down the street.

The carriage driver shrugs and lights a cigarette.

INT. NIGHTCLUB LOUNGE - NIGHT

Malik enters the lounge and looks around. He takes out his
phone and pulls up a text message with a photo attached.
He looks at the photo then scans the room to see an
attractive, dark-skinned woman staring back at him. This is
SANDRA.

Malik walks towards her and smiles broadly. She stands and
gives him a warm hug.

SANDRA
You MUST be Malik. You're WAY cuter than your picture!

MALIK
(laughs)
Thanks. I like to exceed expectations whenever possible.

Sandra smiles flirtatiously and leads him to a seat at a table near the front.

SANDRA
Thanks for agreeing to come. This is probably the last place that allows open mic in the city.

MALIK
Shoot, I love open mics! Guaranteed comedy.

SANDRA
Oh, no, this isn't a comedy one. This is more spoken word.

MALIK
(laughing)
See, that's what I mean! What is "spoken word"?
If they write it down, is it the "written word"?
I mean...

Sandra's eyes narrow at him and we cut to the **MC** (Black man, age not important) on stage.

MC
Welcome, welcome to Open Mic.
This is our 3rd week in a row, and we do want to keep it goin'. PLEASE keep comin' out to support LIVE self-expression. We gon' season and bless this stage before the newbies get started. Give a warm welcome to... LyricSS.

Baltimore-based poet LYRICSS comes to the stage and performs her infamous piece "I'm Not a Damn Vacation."

LYRICSS

I am not a damn vacation / My hips are not the jungle gym / and although it gets wet down below / it is not a water slide / no you cannot come and hide inside of me / so you don't have to face your own reality / I am not a damn vacation / I am a damn good situation
I am the bring me home to momma type / I am not B.E.T., M.T.V., Or any type of video hoe type /I'm the real roll with you sista / the kind that will support her mista /
I am not going to walk behind you / but I will walk beside you / to help you see through any tough situation / because with my street and book education /
I am a damn good package /
but I am not a damn vacation
You cannot use me up and escape / you will not get any frequent flier miles / and I am not redeemable upon your request / I am a long term contract / I'm a house with a deed / the more you invest with me / I appreciate in value /
I add to your assets / I bring residual revenue /
with my vision, ambition, and drive / looking to match and raise you / and place stock in the fact that any seed you plant in me will be nurtured and directed toward the Divinity /
to add to creation and our foundation / because I plan on building using a solid equation / You, me, and God / so if you were just window shopping or needed a break from your current space / keep it moving / because your credit and vision is too short / to be a part of this mission.

The audience snaps, nods, and cheers emphatically as she leaves and the MC returns to the stage.

MC

Well, damn. Open up the mic! First up is a man who calls himself Broken Arrow. Give it up for him.

The audience snaps and claps as **BROKEN ARROW**
(Black man, tall, traditionally handsome) makes his way onto
the stage wearing fatigues and a gold chain.

BROKEN ARROW
I. Am. Broken. I came to do this spoken-
Word because I feel things. Words give me wings.
Wings are delicious and I don't mean to be capricious but
your critiques of me are a bit salacious and I don't feel like
being part of your vicious--
lies. Like flies. Buzzing, surrounding a stinking pile of --

Malik looks pained and is clearly fighting laughter.
Sandra, meanwhile, is totally into it and dying to see where
this is going.

BROKEN ARROW
-- pies. Thought I was gonna say it, didn't you?
But that'd be nasty like a flu. Or a coup,
that we should have against the gov'ment.
Meant to do that but we spent--
our time on frivolous things.
Like chicken wings.
That. Are. Broken.

He walks off to some confused but sympathetic snaps.

Sandra stands up to applaud. She is the only one to do so.

SANDRA
(calling out to him)
You did real good, Day-Day.

Malik looks at her like she is crazy.

MC
Alright, let's get some more woman energy in here.
Rosay, you are up.

ROSAY (Black woman, 30s, brimming with the confidence of a queen) sashays her way up to the stage.

ROSAY
Thank you. This is called, "You Thought."

She breathes deeply, stares ahead intensely, and begins... yelling, basically.

ROSAY
YOU THOUGHT YOU WAS GON' GET AWAY WITH IT.
COMIN' IN HERE WIT'CHA NEW CHICK.
I'MA RHYME MY NEXT LINE WIT 'YOU AIN'T SHIT'...

We see a man attempting to discreetly escape the scene, but she sees him.

ROSAY
OH, DID I STRIKE A NERVE?
NOW YOU GOTTA LEAVE, HUH?

Rosay takes off her shoe and throws it boomerang-style across the room, hitting its target square in the back of the head.

The club patrons collectively "OOOOH!" as he stumbles forward.

CHEATING GUY'S DATE
(*steps forward angrily*)
Hey!!

CHEATING GUY
(turns and yells toward the stage)
Why you gotta do this now?!

ROSAY
Why YOU gotta do this now?

She knocks the mic over and hustles off the stage.

SANDRA
Oh my.

The din of the club increases as Malik pulls out his phone and turns in his seat to start recording.

The Cheating Guy pleads to her, holding his arms out in front of him as she approaches. He's anticipating another flying object.

CHEATING GUY
PEACE! Peace, Rosay, come on! Shit!

Right before she gets to him, he disappears with an audible POP sound.

The club patrons collectively "DAAAMMMNNN!"
Malik, mid-"DAMN" looks up from his phone in awe.

Rosay stands with her mouth open.

CHEATING GUY'S DATE
Did he just pop out?
(turns to random clubgoer)
Did he just pop out?
(turns to Rosay)
Did he just pop out?

The MC recovers the mic and shakes his head.

MC
(quietly)
I hate open mic nights.
(into mic) Come on, y'all, simmer down. It's over.

MALIK
(turns to Sandra, laughing)
I can't believe dude popped out!

Sandra pays him no attention, as she is now feeling the other women's anger at the guy who "popped out" instead of facing the music. She is on an activist mission.

SANDRA
(stands up and starts chanting)
I'M NOT A DAMN VACATION!
I'M NOT A DAMN VACATION!

MC
Aw, hell. Every week wit'chu, Sandra?

Other women in the club start chanting "I'm not a damn vacation!" Most of the men look like they aren't sure what to do.

Malik realizes his chance to escape undetected, and hurries his way out.

FADE TO BLACK.

INT. TEA AND SAMMICHES CAFE - NIGHT

Heartly and Malik are talking over their empty plates, and, obviously, discussing their date fails.

MALIK
At this point, I think I should just go straight for sexual
compatibility. I'm puttin' in a request for a Virgo.

HEARTLY
Well, lemme get an Aries, then.
I can't take another hopeless romantic.

MALIK
You don't appreciate SHIT!

HEARTLY
I do appreciate SHIT, but that was too much!
That was desperation and despair.
YOU don't appreciate shit! You talkin' sexual compatibility--
If you had played your cards right, you coulda had a good
time with ol' girl... eventually.

MALIK
Too easy.

HEARTLY
Oh, please. So why the Virgo, then?

MALIK
I can get some challenge, some mental stimulation...
Then, once the games are done, we can buss it out
and keep it movin'.

HEARTLY
Keep it movin', huh?

MALIK
Yeah, and you want an Aries. They can be aggressive as hell,
and you can't get rid of them so easily.

HEARTLY
Hey... if he plays his cards right,
he can be the maintenance man.

Malik makes a face to indicate he is shocked and intrigued.
Jonathan, who is serving them, returns to the table.

JONATHAN
Y'all good?

MALIK
Yeah, man, we good, thanks.

JONATHAN
Brother, excuse me, but I HAVE to ask you a question...

HEARTLY
(expecting Jonathan to start some mess)
Jonathan... please be polite to my FRIEND.

JONATHAN
I just gotta ask...
Look, I'm a game geek and you look JUST like Master Malik.
If you don't know who he is, I will shut up now.

MALIK
(surprised and impressed)
Wow! You must know your stuff.
(offers his hand)
Nice to meet you, man. What's your name?

JONATHAN
(extremely excited)
I knew it! I knew that was you! Wow, you live here?

Malik nods while Heartly looks confused.

JONATHAN (cont'd)
(remembers Malik's hand)
Sorry, I'm Jonathan. I run the Game Onyx website!
You a legend! But I know you know that. Wow.

HEARTLY
(confused)
Whaaaat...

Jonathan lifts up his sleeve to show a tattoo.

JONATHAN
Look, Miss Heartly!

HEARTLY
I don't... know... what...

Jonathan bounces excitedly back and forth.

JONATHAN
Miss Heartly, Master Malik is the lead programmer and
designer for League of Super Legendary Heroes, the most
popular Massive Multiplayer Online game ever to exist!
He designed the characters, levels, and wrote the script for
the biggest video game ever! This tattoo is of my favorite
faction in the game, the Rogue Dragonslayers!

MALIK
Oh, wow! That means a lot to me, man.

JONATHAN
(starts clearing their dishes)
Ay, anything you need, you let me know.
You wanna come through and make sure you have a table,
just call and let me know.

MALIK
Thanks, I appreciate that.

Jonathan walks away.

Heartly stares at Malik, clearly confused but really interested in knowing what she doesn't know about Malik. He looks at his watch.

MALIK
Welp. I gotta run.
See you when I see you!

He drops some bills on the table and smiles mischievously while she's still in shock. He leaves the cafe quickly.

INT. COFFEE SHOP - DAY

Heartly checks her phone and looks at a previous text from Miss Niecey. "You two are scheduled to meet at Coffee and a Biscuit on Friday at noon. His name is Mark."

When she looks up, a tall, broad, handsome Black man in his late 30s is standing next to her small table, holding two cups. This is **MARK**, her date.

MARK
Addicted to the phone, I see.

Heartly looks up and gives him the 'n-word, please' look.

MARK
You Heartly? I'm Mark.

HEARTLY
Oh. You was 'bout to get cussed out, Mark. I was checking to
make sure I had the day and time right. You're late.

MARK
Nah, I got us some tea.

Mark sets a pair of cups down as he sits at the table.

HEARTLY
(attempted politeness)
I'm a coffee person, actually, but thank you.

MARK
Nah, coffee is bad for you. Drink some tea.
It's a new kind they have.

He picks it up and holds it out to her.

MARK (cont'd)
Besides, you don't want coffee this late.
Tea is better for you after noon.

Heartly takes the tea from him and sits it back on the table.

HEARTLY
If you had just waited and asked, I would have told you
that I didn't like tea, and I could be sitting here having my
afternoon coffee right now.

MARK
You don't even want to try it?

HEARTLY
It is not coffee. I do not want it.
Plus, and please don't take this the wrong way, but I can't
trust a drink that a stranger randomly brings to me.

MARK
(severely offended)
Wait, what'chu think, I'ma poison you?

HEARTLY
You would just take a drink from a stranger?

Mark shakes his head, frustrated.
Heartly attempts to regain her composure. She's clearly
irritated but tries to pull it back.

HEARTLY
Well, the point of this meeting was to see if we wanted to
move forward with a date, right?

MARK
I guess, but you shuttin' me down already!

HEARTLY
You're really this bent out of shape over a drink
that I didn't ask for?

MARK
(cutting her off, agitated)
OK, whatever. Let's just move on.
Where you wanna go for a date?

Heartly is taken aback at his reaction.

Two Black people at a table nearby stand up and hug. They
begin speaking in BLACK AMERICAN SIGN LANGUAGE.

MAN
We're back where we started.

WOMAN
This will always be our spot.

MAN
What about these powers?

WOMAN
They're yours now. They're more powerful than most.

MAN
I love you. Forever and always.

WOMAN
I love you too. I'll miss you.

Person 2 pops out. Person 1 breaks into sobs and rushes off tearfully.

MARK
Dammit, man! I hate that creepy shit!
What are they even doing here?

Heartly thinks he's crazy.

HEARTLY
OK. You're clearly upset. I'm gonna go.

She makes a beeline for the door.

MARK
(calling after her)
Yo, that's not crazy to you?
(to the rest of the coffee shop)
That alien shit ain't crazy to y'all?!

Heartly rushes out of the place and down the street.

INT. MALIK'S APARTMENT -- DAY

Malik has packed a picnic basket and is figuring out how to
carry it, plus a blanket and two camping chairs.
Michael is on the sofa watching a comedy called "You're
That Goose" on TV. We can see and hear the TV screen
in the background with a character screaming the catch
phrase "You're that goose!"

MALIK
Bruh, I'ma need some help to get this to the car.

MICHAEL
Bruh. You ain't even invite me!
Get your own snacks to the car.

MALIK
I ain't invitin' you on my date!

MICHAEL
It's a wine festival! All I gotta do is get out the car.
I bet I can meet a lonely, tipsy free spirit and get some in the
parking lot while you tryna talk your date into first base.

MALIK
Oh, you roll like THAT now?

MICHAEL
(getting up from the sofa)
Man, go ahead on your date. I got work to do anyway.
Meeting with the city government on Monday. May get this
contract and stick around.
Then, I'll check out the fine women in this city.

MALIK
Good plan. Now grab a chair.

They head out the door.

INT. HEARTLY'S APARTMENT -- SAME DAY

Heartly turns on the TV.
A news panel is discussing Notofearths with the **NEWS ANCHOR**, an Anderson Cooper knock-off.

NEWS ANCHOR
"Notofearth" is the term we've come to use for those
not from our planet, but there is still very little we know
about them--other than the lives they lead on Earth.
Every day, more and more of these alien beings are revealing
themselves... by simply popping in and out of existence.

The camera closes in on the News Anchor.

NEWS ANCHOR
Why are they here? Do they mean us harm?
Where are they from? What information or technology can
they share with us? In today's segment, we'll hear from ex-
perts and from the most vocal Notofearth representative.

The camera pulls back to show all three members of the
panel.

The **NOTOFEARTH REPRESENTATIVE** is a very tall,
dark-skinned, handsome, intelligent-looking man wearing
glasses and an expensive suit. He is clearly taller than -- and
"above"-- the rest of the panel.

FIRST PANELIST
We cannot trust people who are not even people...who would
come to OUR planet and not even offer the technology to
teleport in and out like they do.

NOTOFEARTH REP
Many of us are here on research missions, some of us are on
vacation to experience life as a human--

SECOND PANELIST
(cuts him off)
A human experience, but no one wants to talk--
I'm gonna talk about it -- but no one wants to talk about the
fact that ALL of these aliens popping in and out of the place
all the time are Black.

NOTOFEARTH REP
We prefer the term 'Notofearth,' thank you.

NEWS ANCHOR
What evidence do you have that all Notofearths are Black?

SECOND PANELIST
Have you ever seen any other type of person just pop out of
existence? Anyone who has ever reported a person or people
popping out or in...they're all African American.

NOTOFEARTH REP
Oh, and you just know they're AMERICAN, too, huh?

SECOND PANELIST
(cutting him off)
SO IT'S TRUE! THEY ARE ALL BLACK!!

NOTOFEARTH REP
Define "Black."

FIRST PANELIST
This kind of arrogance, this deliberate avoidance
of important questions...is what leads to distrust of these
(sarcastically) Notofearths.
We're anticipating another climate-related disaster,

but these people--or whatever--VACATION here.
They can travel between planets but they won't offer us any
help? They won't offer to take us Out There with them?

NOTOFEARTH REP
You just said we can't be trusted, so why would you listen to
us, or come with us *(finger quotes)* "Out There" as you say?

FIRST PANELIST
You're not helping the case by not answering
some very important questions.

NOTOFEARTH REP
What case? Your case? My case is fine.

SECOND PANELIST
WHERE ARE YOU FROM?

NEWS ANCHOR
Do you all invite people to go with you to
where you come from?

NOTOFEARTH REP
Yes.

SECOND PANELIST
But only BLACK people, right?

NOTOFEARTH REP
Oh, so it's not about sharing TECHNOLOGY anymore, huh?
(laughs)

SECOND PANELIST
That is RACIST!

NOTOFEARTH REP
Man...

The Notofearth Representative shakes his head and pops out. His mic falls into the chair.

FIRST PANELIST
This is why nobody likes them.
That popping out when they don't want to engage...

Heartly shuts off the TV.

HEARTLY
Taneefa.

A Black woman's voice answers through a digital assistant.

TANEEFA THE ROBOT
Yes ma'am?

HEARTLY
Play my "Getaway" Playlist.

She walks over to the window as we hear "ZOOM" by the Commodores. She stares out and up longingly into a beautiful blue sky.

FADE TO:

EXT. - WINE FESTIVAL AT A PARK - SAME DAY

A shot of a beautiful blue sky establishes the peaceful, fun vibe of the Wine Festival.

Malik is walking beside his date, **DONNA**, who is carrying one chair while he carries the other chair, the blanket, and the picnic basket. The music blends into a regg'go (reggae/go-go) cover of "ZOOM" as we see and hear Ras Lidj & Deep Band playing it on stage.

As they enter, Donna is more than happy to point out the various sights and sounds.

DONNA
Ok, so, over there we've got the stage. Looks like it's a go-go band, so all them heads'll be making there way over there.

She looks to the left, and a short distance away is where people are gathering to taste the wines.

DONNA (cont'd)
Alright, that must be the wine tasting tent.
Now, since you're new at this, I'm gonna warn you.
Pace yourself. Don't get loaded your first time through or else you'll be "that guy."

MALIK
(eye roll)
It's wine.

DONNA
Suit yourself.
(pointing with her chin) Hmm, over there is where most of your singles start to mingle and hook up.
That's always hilarious to watch.

Malik shifts the heavy gear he's carrying.

MALIK
Ok, ok, and where's the spot where
we're setting all this stuff down?

Donna looks around quickly, assessing the area.

DONNA
Let's see, our best vantage point for easy access to wine and a view of all the ridiculousness is gonna be...

She scans again, then points to a small hill above them.

DONNA (cont'd)
There!

Malik makes his way over and sets the chairs and basket down.

MALIK
All right! Let's drink!

DONNA
You're awfully eager to get some alcohol in your system, aren't you?

MALIK
Yes. Yes I am.

They laugh.

MALIK
Seriously, though, you hold down the fort, I'll bring us back some wine.

Donna shakes her head negatively.

DONNA
That's not how this works. We can leave our stuff here and go. The point of the festival is to sample things. You wouldn't be able to bring me back all the things I want to try.

Malik shrugs and they start toward the wine tent.

CUT TO:

EXT. WINE TENT - MOMENTS LATER

MONTAGE:
Malik and Donna joke with each other as they sip glass

after glass of different wines. Malik is getting lit; Donna is keeping it cool.

MALIK
HOW HAVE I NEVER BEEN TO A WINE TASTING
THINGY BEFORE? THIS IS THE BEST EXPERIENCE OF
MY LIFE. SO MUCH TASTY BEVERAGES!

DONNA
Ok, you're a little on the loud side.
You're at a 10, I need you to come down to like a 4.

Malik looks at her blankly, then tries to compose himself.

MALIK
(whispering loudly)
OK MY BAD SORRY.
NOT TRYING TO EMBARRASS YOU OR NOTHIN'.

DONNA
Mmhmm. Come on Drinky. Let's go sit for a bit.

Donna starts to lead him back to their spot, but Malik resists.

MALIK
NO, WAIT, THE BAND. WE SHOULD DANCE AND SHIT.

Malik grabs her by the hand and drags her toward the stage, pushing his way through the crowd toward the front. Donna tries to pull away but Malik tugs harder.

DONNA
Seriously, I need you to let go.
You're a little too aggressive right now.

MALIK
DON'T BE A WET BLANKET GIRL, THIS SHIT IS LITTY.

DONNA
I SAID LET GO.

Malik releases her, surprised at her voice. Bystanders also turn towards them. A few men step forward, ready to step in and handle Malik.

MALIK
YOU...JUST...DON'T KNOW HOW...FUN...CONTROLLING EVERYTHING AND...AND...MAKING IT ALL...ABOUT...

Malik wobbles. He's gonna be sick but he's trying to hold back.

MALIK
Shit. Gonna be...ah fuh--

Malik vomits everywhere. The now gathered crowd gasps and recoils. Donna walks away and pulls out her phone to make a call.

DONNA
(*into phone*)
Gurl. You ain't gonna believe this shit.
Come pick me up.

Donna looks back at Malik, shakes her head, and keeps walking away.

INT. MALIK'S APARTMENT - THE NEXT DAY

Malik nurses a hangover while watching the local news with

the sound turned down. There's a knock at the door.

MALIK
I think it's open.

The doorknob jiggles but nothing happens.

MALIK
(groans) Nooo...

He slides off the couch and drags himself to his feet, finally
reaching the door after a few more impatient knocks.
He unlocks and opens the door. It's Heartly.

MALIK
(mutters unintelligibly)

Heartly holds up two cups of coffee as she enters.

HEARTLY
Damn. What did you get into last night?

Malik carefully settles back onto the couch.

MALIK
I got into too much wine, apparently.

HEARTLY
Amateur. Didn't nobody warn you to pace yourself?

Heartly sits next to him and hands him a coffee.

MALIK
She did. I ain't listen and puked all over everything after
looking like an ign'ant a-hole.

HEARTLY
What in the entire hell?

MALIK
It wasn't gonna work out anyway. She was all about having
things her way, seemed like a know-it-all.
But she was right. I should've paced myself.
Thank goodness it didn't end up on --

Heartly has already pulled out her phone and hit YouTube.
Sure enough, there's the clip, "Man gets dumped at Local
Wine Fest, pukes."

HEARTLY
Oh damn...that's a lot of puke.
Still can't really tell it's you, though. I mean, I can...

Malik groans and covers his face with a pillow. Heartly is
shaking her head.

MALIK
(from under the pillow)
How'd you do?

HEARTLY
What?
(snatches the pillow)

MALIK
Miss Niecey's magic pick for you?

HEARTLY
HOLY MOLY. This fool.
We ain't even make it 5 minutes.

MALIK
So no maintenance man?

Heartly gives him the most sincere I'm-not-kidding face ever.

HEARTLY
He comes over to me with a tea--already bought--but didn't even ask me what I wanted. Then had the nerve to get mad when I called him out on it--

Malik rolls his eyes.

HEARTLY (cont'd)
--and THEN he launched into some xenophobic mess about Notofearths and I was just done.

Malik slowly holds up a finger to interject, but changes his mind.

HEARTLY (cont'd)
Come on! That's that bullshit! It's one thing if you know someone well enough to know what they like and THEN get it for them. It's a whole other thing to just decide you gon' buy somebody something without even knowing them. That's how people get roofied!

Malik is still looking at her, saying nothing.

HEARTLY (cont'd)
AND THEN TO BE XENOPHOBIC--
SPECIESIST -- WHATEVER THE HELL,
AND NOT EXPECT ME TO GET MAD??

Malik is feigning terror as Heartly regains her composure.

HEARTLY (cont'd)
Anyway. I guess you ain't goin' nowhere today.

MALIK
(*weakly shaking his head*)
Mm-mm.

HEARTLY
Where your roommate?

MALIK
Why?

HEARTLY
(*annoyed*)
Is he here? I need to know if I'm gettin' comfortable.

MALIK
You ain't gettin' nekkid, calm down.

HEARTLY
CALM DOWN?!

MALIK
If you gon' keep bein' loud, you gotta leave.

HEARTLY
(*gets up and walks toward the bedrooms*)
Hello?? Roommate?

MALIK
He's out of town. Damn.

HEARTLY
(*comes back to the sofa*)
I'm ordering lunch. Why is he always outta town?

MALIK
You can ask him when you meet him.

He turns over and puts the pillow over his head.

FADE TO BLACK.

EXT. OUTSIDE SOMEWHERE - DAY
MAN-ON-THE-STREET INTERVIEWS

"I'LL TAKE YOU THERE" by The Staples Singers plays softly
while several Black people riff in response to the question
of whether they would go "Out There" with the
Notofearths if they were invited.

PERSON ON STREET 1
I heard some people say they was goin' Out There, but I'm
like, out where? Like, where you goin?

PERSON ON STREET 2
I don't know, man... I heard they only invitin' Black people?

PERSON ON STREET 3
Yeah, I'd go. Especially if I could come back.
But then again, Mother Earth seem kinda mad at us, so...

PERSON ON STREET 1
If they would say whether they takin' us to a planet, another
dimension... I mean, what?

PERSON ON STREET 2
That sound like a trap...

PERSON ON STREET 3
If they Black like us, we should try to build
for-real universal bonds, right?

CUT TO BLACK.

INT. HEARTLY'S AND MALIK'S APARTMENTS - EVENING

Split screen with both Heartly and Malik looking into their laptop screens. We hear typing on keyboards and then their simultaneous clicks.

CUT TO:

A video invitation from a Miss Niecey employee speaking in front of a green screen-assisted background about an event called "MERCURY RETROGRADE ROMP & STOMP." Once again, Kato Hammond's "GO-GO ZODIAC THEME" song plays.

MISS NIECEY'S EMPLOYEE
(ON VIDEO)
It's Miss Niecey's MERCURY RETROGRADE
ROMP & STOMP!
If you're receiving this, Miss Niecey has chosen YOU
to meet other like-minded, SINGLE people,
THIS Saturday night at 8pm.
Open and curious minds are most welcome.
BE THERRRRRRE!

The video is interspersed with the split screen of Heartly and Malik staring into their laptops, amazed.

CUT TO:

INT. MISS NIECEY'S MERCURY RETROGRADE ROMP & STOMP - NIGHT

Heartly enters the party. The space itself is not fancy, but the party is jumping. DJ Heat's "CITY GIRL (ft. Styme & Reece P)" plays as we make our way through the party, seeing how much fun everyone is having.

People are wearing wide ribbons in different colors that hang around their necks, each imprinted with a zodiac sign.

Heartly spots the table where these ribbons are being distributed and makes her way over.

An interesting **CAPRICORN** woman (Black, 30s, thin, unique look) is handing them out.

> **CAPRICORN**
> Hi! Welcome! And you are a...?

> **HEARTLY**
> *(extends hand for handshake)*
> Heartly!

> **CAPRICORN**
> *(leans in closer to hear better)*
> I'm sorry?

> **HEARTLY**
> HEART-LEE. Like a heart!

Heartly makes a heart shape with her hands. Behind her, Malik approaches, then leans past her and speaks to the Capricorn.

> **MALIK**
> Scorpio!

The Capricorn smiles and hands him a Scorpio ribbon.

> **HEARTLY**
> *(embarrassed)* Oh. Gemini.

The Capricorn hands Heartly her Gemini tag and smiles with interest.

CAPRICORN
It's nice to meet you, Heartly, like a heart.

HEARTLY
(blushes)
You too.

Malik faces the crowd, puts his ribbon around his neck, and smiles, captivated by what's guaranteed to be a fun night for him. Heartly's gaze lingers on the Capricorn before turning to Malik.

MALIK
Looks like it's gonna be a good night!

HEARTLY
Right?

MALIK
(seeing the bar across the room)
Star Bar?

HEARTLY
Please.

They make their way to the bar as someone else reaches the Capricorn to receive their zodiac ribbon.

From the bar, Heartly and Malik see Miss Niecey take the stage and pick up the mic.

MISS NIECEY
Thank you all for coming! We are so happy to have you here!
Miss Niecey's is a special singles' community
that wouldn't be what it is without YOU.
If you are recently joining us, please know that
we believe in intergalactic solidarity.

We do have some Notofearth friends joining us, Amen, Ase?

Voices in the crowd "amen" and "ah-shay" in response.

MISS NIECEY
If you AIN'T from Planet Earth...make some noiiiiiise!!

A significant portion of the crowd makes noise while the others look around, impressed and excited at the energy in the room.

Heartly looks back at the Capricorn and realizes she's cheering as well. The music kicks back in and the party goes back into full swing.

EXT. A WALKING/RUNNING TRAIL IN THE PARK - DAY

Heartly and Capricorn are finishing a brisk walk/run on a trail in a park. They are clearly enjoying each other's company.

CAPRICORN
Alright, cool down's over. I need to rest.

HEARTLY
Rest? Don't you people have powers?

CAPRICORN
What do you mean, "you people?"

HEARTLY
Oh...oh my goodness...oh, I'm so sorry.

CAPRICORN
(smiles)
Just teasing.

HEARTLY
(relieved, then playfully irritated)
You ain't right!
But, like, seriously, don't you all have powers
so you don't get tired or whatever like we do?

They sit on a bench.

CAPRICORN
What do powers have to do with being tired?
I don't trust any being that doesn't get tired.

HEARTLY
(nodding)
I hear you.

Heartly sips water to give herself time to collect her
thoughts.

HEARTLY (cont'd)
Beings. Wow.
So...like, what other types of beings have you met?
Out There? And how far away do you actually live?

CAPRICORN
I live up the street from here.

HEARTLY
Yeah, but, like, you know--

CAPRICORN
But like, where am I really from? Am I gonna kill you in your
sleep? But, more importantly, what's sex like with me?
Is it so good that you'd take the chance
that I'd kill you in your sleep?

Heartly looks embarrassed.

HEARTLY
Come on...I'm not like that!

Capricorn gives her a look.

HEARTLY (cont'd)
So I can't ask you any questions?

CAPRICORN
Sure, you can ask questions. About ME. There's getting to know me, and there's treating me like a science project.

HEARTLY
Isn't you being Notofearth a big part of who you are? Like how being Black is a big part of who I am on Earth?

CAPRICORN
(disappointed in Heartly's insistence)
I guess it is.

HEARTLY
Don't people ask you questions all the time?
(finally understanding the annoyance)
Oh.

STACEY (O.S.)
Heartly!

Heartly and Capricorn look toward the voice to see Stacey running toward them. She has also been jogging.

STACEY
Hey woman!

She stops in front of them and speaks to the Capricorn.

STACEY
Hello!

CAPRICORN
(pleasant)
Hi.

Stacey addresses Heartly with her hands on her hips.

STACEY
You puttin' that new outfit to good use or you just flexin'?

HEARTLY
Don't roll up on me startin' nothin', I'm on a date!

Stacey raises an eyebrow and smirks at Capricorn, who returns the look with a slight negative shake of the head, indicating that their "date" is no big deal.

STACEY
You are so sensitive. Get it together!

CAPRICORN
(laughing)
Oh, you DO have friends!

Heartly gasps, offended.

STACEY
(to Capricorn)
And the struggle is REAL, sis.

HEARTLY
You know what, y'all have fun running together.
I will go where I'm appreciated.

Heartly starts to get up.

STACEY
Oh, sit down, you big baby.

CAPRICORN
We were just finishing up. I need to get home.

HEARTLY
Already?

Capricorn gets up.

CAPRICORN
We've been out here a while.
(apologetic) I gotta get home.

HEARTLY
(standing up)
But...

STACEY
You two say goodbyes.
(to Heartly)
I'll meet you in the parking lot.
(to Capricorn)
It was nice meeting you.

CAPRICORN
Same here.

Stacey walks away.

Heartly steps forward, closer to Capricorn with a look and body language indicating that she knows it's not going to work out but there's no hard feelings.

CAPRICORN
I'm sorry too.

HEARTLY
YOU CAN READ MINDS?!

CAPRICORN
(laughs)
I should take a picture of the look on your face right now.
Priceless!

HEARTLY
Wait! Are you messing with me?

CAPRICORN
You are adorbs.

HEARTLY
Ha. Ha.

CAPRICORN
Give me my hug so I can go.
(as if to a child) Come on.

They embrace.

CAPRICORN

You know... If we're hugging when I pop out, you go with me.

Heartly hugs her tighter and her eyes dart back in forth in anticipation.

CAPRICORN
(kindly) Aww. You wanna go, don't you?

Heartly pulls away.

HEARTLY
That's not funny.

CAPRICORN
It is funny. And possible. Just not with me.

Heartly looks dejected. Capricorn just smiles.

HEARTLY
So, how do we say goodbye?
You gonna pop out, or...?

CAPRICORN
Well, we just hugged so I'm gonna...
(gestures over her shoulder)
...start walking to my house. Over there. See ya!

Capricorn walks away and Heartly watches her for two seconds.

HEARTLY
See ya.

Heartly walks up to Stacey.

STACEY
You ok?

HEARTLY
Yup.

STACEY
I'll take you for a smoothie. My treat. How's that?

HEARTLY
Homemade. With vodka.

FADE TO:

INT. HEARTLY'S APARTMENT - NIGHT

Stacey and Heartly are painting their toenails, listening to music and sipping wine.

STACEY

So you're really not gonna bring up Miss Thing, huh?

Heartly sighs loudly.

STACEY (cont'd)

Or all those texts lately about you being on a date and letting
me know where you'd be, just in case...

Heartly sighs again, louder.

STACEY (cont'd)

I think I've been patient enough, haven't I?

HEARTLY

Yeah, and you also tried to block me today!

STACEY

What's for you is FOR YOU, and there's nothing I could do to
block your blessing--if it's actually a blessing.

Heartly sighs again. Stacey looks at her smugly, sipping her
wine.

HEARTLY

I joined a dating service, ok?

STACEY

(clearly shocked)

Dating service??

HEARTLY

Yes. Dating. Service.

STACEY
How you gon' swear off dating after the fake Doctor Feel
Good and then join A DATING SERVICE?

HEARTLY
It was on a dare.
Malik, my friend I told you about, he joined too.

STACEY
On a dare?

HEARTLY
Yeah, we saw this commercial on TV
about a place that matches you by your Zodiac sign.
(shrugs)
We called and joined.

STACEY
Zodiac sign? That's not even real!

Heartly stands and stretches, waddles over to get another
bottle of wine while keeping her toes from touching the
floor, then sits back down.

HEARTLY
It doesn't have to be real. It's--

She searches for words while shaking a bottle of nail polish.

STACEY
Yes?

Heartly paints a nail.

STACEY
Hello??

HEARTLY
You know the Notofearths, right?

STACEY
(*looking up to the ceiling*)
Dear Lord, why...?

HEARTLY
(*sadly*)
Please don't turn into Reverend Killjoy right now.

STACEY
Not. Of. Earth.
Zodiac: Not. Of. God.

HEARTLY
See...this is whyyy...

STACEY
Look, I really want you to be ok. Ok?
A lot of people are going through it right now.
Maybe you should join a support group,
or see a therapist again--

HEARTLY
Been there, done that.
I'm doing what I want to do.
I'm grown. I don't need a mother.

Stacey shakes her head.

STACEY
Speaking of your mother, you talk to her lately?

HEARTLY
I can't put myself through it again, Stace.
Going to therapy helped me be ok with cutting her off.

You know she breaks me. Every time.
I deserve better. I deserve to be happy.

STACEY
I know. I'm sorry.

HEARTLY
Maybe what I need is...Out There.
I need something better, something more than this.

STACEY
OH, LORD!
Now you wanna go Out There with them?
Out where? Tell me that.

HEARTLY
I'm researching it!
Look...

Heartly reaches for a copy of *ThinkPiece* magazine on a nearby table. She opens it and we can see the cover, featuring the Notofearth Representative, Chief, from the news segment she watched. One of the cover lines reads "Master Malik, Gaming's Newest Hero."

She turns to a page and begins to read out loud.

HEARTLY
(reading)
"Where we come from, there is peace because we serve the elements. Water, light, terra, and others that are not understood on Earth, we understand. Life force is sacred. Those who serve Self over Life face immediate karmic retribution..."

STACEY
(cutting her off)
It could be one giant hoax! People are zappin' in and out of
reality? People with powers that won't help us? And now
they're offering us a way off the planet? None of us have gone
and come back to say it's safe. It could be one big ass trap!

HEARTLY
Trap for what?

STACEY
Who knows what?

Heartly sits back and exhales deeply.

HEARTLY
THAT is what research is for.
I didn't say I was leaving tomorrow. I'm just looking into it.

STACEY
You're just looking into it. Not too long ago you were trying
to convince me to go into business with you, then you start
Zodiac dating, and now this.
Do you even know what you want?

Heartly looks wounded.

STACEY
Do you even KNOW any aliens?

HEARTLY
I don't like that word. Neither do they.
Notofearths are everywhere. I know how to make friends and
meet people. That girl from earlier, for one.

STACEY
They ain't people.

HEARTLY
Well, I wanna see. I wanna check it out.

STACEY
Heartly.

Stacey knows she won't win. There's nothing she can say once Heartly has made a decision.

STACEY (cont'd)
Tell me EVERYTHING you find out.

HEARTLY
I knew you believed in me.

Heartly looks up toward the window and sees what looks like two brightly lit forms flying and playing around in the sky.

HEARTLY
Look!

They get up and run to the window. Stacey takes pictures with her cell.

STACEY
Everything is SO WEIRD now.

INT. - UPSCALE RESTAURANT - DAY

Heartly and her **COWORKER** (white woman, 40s) are at lunch in a fancy restaurant with a bar.

COWORKER
We are here to LISTEN. We don't want to give this guy any
indication that we need software or that our servers are a
complete mess. None of that. Just let him make his sales
pitch, we get a free lunch, and...it's after noon, so...

HEARTLY
(*smiles*)
The usual.

COWORKER
(*smiles*)
The usual.

Heartly makes her way to the bar. As she walks, she locks
eyes with a handsome man (**MICHAEL**) and walks straight
toward him. He takes her in, with interest, as she walks.

When she reaches him, she turns away from him to the
BARTENDER 2, a woman who is familiar with Heartly and
her usual order.

BARTENDER 2
Hey there, Miss.

HEARTLY
Hey Boo. The usual.

BARTENDER 2
Coming right up!

MICHAEL
Oh, "the usual," huh?

Heartly turns toward Michael, playing it cool, though she is
definitely attracted to him.

HEARTLY
Are you a regular here?

MICHAEL
No, I'm new in town.

There's an undeniable, palpable attraction between them.
They can barely stray from their mutual locked gaze.

HEARTLY
Really? You have friends or family here?

MICHAEL
Some family. I could use some more friends though.

He hands her a business card.

MICHAEL
I'm here on business, but...keep in touch.

Heartly takes the card and begins to read it.

HEARTLY
Michael--

Her coworker pops up behind them.

COWORKER
You found him! Michael, good to see you!
(*shakes his hand excitedly*)
We're right over here.
(*gestures toward their table*)
What're you drinking, water?

MICHAEL
Well, no one told me about "The Usual."

COWORKER
You two have a seat, I'll get our "usuals."

Michael, being a gentleman, lets Heartly walk in front of him to lead the way. He admires the view from behind. They sit facing each other.

Heartly attempts to pretend as if the work connection ruins any chance of them hooking up.

HEARTLY
Darn it.

Michael gives her the same look.

MICHAEL
Yeah. Darn it.

Heartly's Coworker returns with the drinks.

COWORKER
Alrighty then! Let's talk software!

MICHAEL
Okay, but I'll definitely need more than a liquid lunch.

COWORKER
Right, yes! Let's order!

Heartly passes the menu to Michael and they lock eyes again.

CUT TO:

EXT. - MICHAEL'S CAR - LATER THAT NIGHT

Heartly and Michael are making out in the front seat of his car. It's hot and heavy.

"FREE" by Deniece Williams is playing on the radio. Michael stops at the sound of one of his favorite songs, pushing her back, gently.

MICHAEL
(sits back, out of breath)
Whew! This song WOULD play right now.

HEARTLY
Let me find out you're sentimental.

MICHAEL
This song reminds me of the best birthday I ever had.

HEARTLY
Oh? A woman?

MICHAEL
Nah, just the vibe. I'm still chasing that high.

HEARTLY
When is your birthday, anyway?

MICHAEL
January.

HEARTLY
(makes a face)
Capricorn?

MICHAEL
Nah, Aquarius.
(returns her twisted face)
You one of them Zodiac people?

HEARTLY
Uh, no, just asking.

MICHAEL
(*skeptical*) Ok.
Oh, your lipstick.

Heartly pulls down the visor to look in the mirror.
Her lipstick is smeared up the side of her face.

HEARTLY
Oops.

She reaches down to remove a tissue and lipstick from her
purse. She cleans her face and reapplies it while Michael
checks his face. He gets a napkin from his console and
wipes his mouth.

HEARTLY
Too bad. It was such a nice shade on you.

MICHAEL
You can paint me up again later.

Michael unlocks the doors. They exchange glances again,
intense heat between them. They deny their impulses and
get out of the car.

INT. COMEDY CLUB - SAME NIGHT, MOMENTS LATER

Heartly and Michael are sitting near the front of the stage
and a **COMEDIAN** is on the mic.
The audience is in stitches.

COMEDIAN
I can tell who's on a date and who's in a relationship.

(looks at a couple)
Y'all look like you like each other, so that's a date.
(looks at another couple)
She done had a attitude since I got up here,
so that's a relationship. What did you do, man?
How you gonna make your woman mad before coming to a
comedy show? Now I gotta work extra hard.
(looks at Heartly and Michael)
You two look like you IN LOVE. Y'all in love?

Heartly shakes her head "no."

MICHAEL
First date.

The audience oohs and ahhs to tease them.

COMEDIAN
First date?? Wow, y'all glowin' though.
Y'all smashin' tonight?

Michael and Heartly laugh in embarrassment.

COMEDIAN
(to audience)
Let me explain something to y'all--
since people like to get caught up judging women by what
they want to do on a first date. We need to enjoy ourselves
while we can. Remember when the thought of aliens was
scary? Because what did we think?
That they want to take over Earth! Guess what?
They don't want this shit! They take a vacation and be OUT.
(to Heartly and Michael)
Y'all need to get it in while you can. Fuck that single shit! If
y'all tryna fall in love, DO IT! Have some sex! A lot!
TONIGHT! Promise us y'all gonna do it!
For the human race, come on!

Michael and Heartly laugh and look at each other as the crowd goes wild.

CUT TO:

INT. MALIK'S APARTMENT - NEXT MORNING

Malik reclines on the couch watching TV and eating cereal. On the screen, two Black women are discussing a new book.

TV HOST

Our guest today is Lola Swann, the author of *Booty Balance*. This book is taking the Singles' Movement by storm. You may already be a fan of Lola Swann from her podcast...

Michael enters the living room, groggy but amused. It's clearly been a good night.

MALIK

ALL NIGHT LONG, huh?

MICHAEL

(plops down on the couch)
I think I may like it here after all.

MALIK

Did you at least take a damn shower?

MICHAEL

Nope! Eff yo' couch!

Michael shimmies his butt into the cushions disrespectfully.

MALIK

Ugh...you nasty!

Malik gestures toward the TV.

MALIK
See, this what *I'm* talkin' 'bout.
While you be out here tryna settle down.

MICHAEL
(annoyed) What?

CUT TO:

INT. TV SHOW SET WITH HOST AND AUTHOR

AUTHOR LOLA SWANN
We may, in fact, be doing ourselves a disservice by settling
down with just one person. Especially because this planet
may not last much longer.

TV HOST
What about the MANY people who still believe in
true love, marriage, families?
A love to enjoy in these end-of-days times?

AUTHOR LOLA SWANN
People have been talking about the "end-of-days" for
centuries now. We're still here. But, just in case this is it,
many, many people are finding comfort in committing to a
Single Life. At least through their 30s.
Some through their 40s, and even 50s.

TV HOST
What if they have children? People usually want to have a
complete family.

AUTHOR LOLA SWANN
(shrugs)
Children happen.

AUTHOR LOLA SWANN (cont'd)
But, for those of us - with and without children - who are
committed to the Singles' Movement, we need systems that
help us pick the best matches for our life phases.

CUT BACK TO:

INT. MALIK'S APARTMENT

MICHAEL
Children hap--

MALIK
Shh! SHHHH!

CUT BACK TO:

INT. TV SHOW SET WITH HOST AND AUTHOR

TV HOST
Life phases?

AUTHOR LOLA SWANN
Think about it. At different phases, you're into different
things, and many times, you date based on those interests.
After a breakup, when you look back at what went wrong...
you still realize that the other person gave you two things:
Booty and a common interest.

Malik nods in agreement and Michael shakes his head in
disbelief. The TV Host looks as if she is sincerely trying to
understand.

AUTHOR LOLA SWANN (cont'd)
According to my Single Societal Orientation, two people
being honest about that sex and that common interest allows
a strong - albeit temporary - relationship. It's never going to

last, but then again, neither is our planet.

TV HOST
(trying her best to keep a neutral face)
So let's see some of these booty matches--
uh, Booty Balances that your book suggests.

The TV Host reads a list displayed as an onscreen graphic.

TV HOST
Bougie Booty. Black Power Booty. Nerdy Booty.
Corporate Booty. Artsy Booty. Boozy Booty. Sporty Booty.
Shopping Booty.
And in your book, there are even more...

CUT BACK TO:

INT. MALIK'S APARTMENT

We see the TV screen, on which the author looks quite
smug and proud of herself.

MICHAEL
WHAT??

MALIK
You could use this book.

MICHAEL
How you figure that?

MALIK
You ain't been in town five minutes and already
met a woman you stayed out all night with.
THAT is the single life. AND you don't LIVE here.
You gettin' the booty. You need the balance.

MICHAEL
How you know what I'm getting and what I need?

MALIK
Women in this area ain't goin' for all that
mushy stuff no more. That's what they talkin' about.
Singles' Movement got 'em.

MICHAEL
And you speak for every woman in town, huh?

MALIK
Fine. Don't take my word for it.

Malik puts his hand on Michael's shoulder as though he's about to say something wise. Sage advice is coming.

MALIK
Just...don't start pushing up too quick. Give her some space.

MICHAEL
(*offended*) I ain't no loser-ass dude, bruh!

MALIK
(*mocking*) OKAY, BRUH.
I'm just saying, this single life is all about equal opportunity.

MICHAEL
Uh huh.

MALIK
Give HER the opportunity to make the next move.
Did she seem clingy?

Malik looks dramatically toward the door, grabbing the couch in mock fear.

MALIK
She ain't gonna show up here, is she?

Michael yawns, rising from the couch and stretching.

MICHAEL
Let me go get some shut-eye.

MALIK
Nah, stay woke.

MICHAEL
You so woke, you high. On some bullshit.

Michael walks away toward his room.

MALIK
That was corny, bruh.
(calling out after Michael)
Aye, can you bring me that cereal on the counter?

MICHAEL
(without turning around)
Nope!

INT. MICHAEL'S ROOM - MOMENTS LATER

Michael is lying on his bed. We see the back of his head. He turns toward the camera and reaches for his phone. He starts to call, then stops.

Instead, he opens the text messages and starts to type something to Heartly. Then, he hears Malik's voice.

MALIK (V.O.)
Give HER the opportunity to make the next move. SUCKA.

Michael closes the message app and tosses the phone aside.

CUT TO:

INT. HEARTLY'S APARTMENT/STACEY'S HOUSE - MORNING

Heartly lies in her bed looking at her phone, wearing her reading glasses. She opens the message app to text Michael. Three dots appear for a few seconds. She giggles with anticipation.

The three dots disappear. Then nothing.

She calls Stacey. We go back and forth between the two in their homes, talking on the phone to each other.

STACEY
You up early, girl, or getting in late?

HEARTLY
Both? *(She takes off her glasses)*
Girl. This man... he's a delight.

STACEY
Uh oh.
You only use that word for people you really feelin'.
That's saying a lot.

HEARTLY
But I mean, I definitely like him.
We vibe, there's an undeniable attraction.
The things he can do with his--

STACEY
(cutting her off abruptly)
Yeah, yeah, I don't need to be a party to your debauchery.
Look, you're still a lady, right?
As crazy as you are, you still have SOME standards, right?

Heartly sits up in bed.

HEARTLY
Yes, obviously.

STACEY
Then let a man be a man.
He needs to be the one to make the next move.
He needs to call you, make the next date, show you he 'bout
that life and that you aren't just some random-ass … ass.

Heartly nods in agreement.

HEARTLY
I AM a LADY. You are absolutely right.
He need to show me something other than what dat mouf do.

STACEY
Ew. Goodbye. Good luck.

Heartly ends the call and tosses the phone aside.

FADE TO BLACK.

FADE IN:

INT. HEARTLY'S APARTMENT - EVENING

Malik, still in his coat after arriving at Heartly's place, is

taking food out of a bag and putting items on Heartly's
dining table. Heartly is in the middle of a rant.

HEARTLY
--The girl clearly just hates herself.
I told you about her weave. You ever seen a weave just give
up on life? I DID.
She is just the Mother Teresa of basic bitches.

Malik silently busies himself with the groceries as Heartly
continues.

HEARTLY
It's been two years and we don't even speak words to each
other in meetings, in the hallway, nothing. It would take a
burning bush, a pillar of fire, a dove, the physical presence of
the Lord Himself for me to acknowledge that ho.
I was triggered. I felt a sliver of compassion because she is
obviously going through something, but...

Malik sets down a blender. Then he triumphantly sets down
a bowl.

MALIK
Guacamole. Homemade.

HEARTLY
SHUT THE FRONT DOOR! GIMME!

Heartly runs to the kitchen drawer and grabs a spoon to
taste the guacamole.

HEARTLY
Mmmmmmmmm...oh my worrrrdddd.

Malik is pleased with himself and Heartly is clearly happy.
They take the food to the living room.

MALIK
What time is it?

HEARTLY
We still got a few minutes.

Heartly grabs the remote and turns on the TV as they sit on the couch.

We see:
- A trailer for the new Sean Short action movie *Wheeled Warrior* featuring a vigilante hero who specializes in martial arts. The scene opens on a flyover of the city as the movie trailer guy voice kicks in:

TRAILER VOICEOVER
In a world where crime is rampant and no one dares to act...

The scene cuts to a dark alley, where a pair of thugs approach a man in a wheelchair from behind.

TRAILER VOICEOVER
...one man dares to turn the wheels...OF JUSTICE.

THUG #1 grabs the man in the wheelchair by the shoulder. A gloved hand reaches over his shoulder and breaks the Thug's hand, then flips him over.

The man in the chair whirls around to reveal SEAN SHORT, THE **WHEELED WARRIOR**, in superhero gear. THUG #2 shrinks in fear as the Wheeled Warrior rolls toward him, extending a collapsible bo staff.

WHEELED WARRIOR
Let's go for a spin.

The Wheeled Warrior spins the bo and clips the Thug's legs

from under him, flipping him into the air. He lands hard and finds the staff at his neck. The camera pans up to the Wheeled Warrior's face. He smirks.

WHEELED WARRIOR
Justice isn't blind...it's capable.

The scene cuts to a police chief screaming at some officers.

POLICE CHIEF
This wheeled vigilante is beating the tar out of the city's criminals and you geniuses can't figure it out?
He's rolling right under our noses!

We then find ourselves in the Wheeled Warrior's Dojo.

SENSEI
Your training is complete.
You're the deadliest of any of my students.

Sean bows to his Sensei.

Cut to an action packed gunfight between a **DETECTIVE** (woman, 30s) and a group of thugs. The Wheeled Warrior enters the room.

DETECTIVE
Sean, no! What are you doing?

WHEELED WARRIOR
Dirty work.

Sean rolls through the gunfight deflecting bullets with his staff and taking thugs out one by one, efficient and deadly.

The Detective steps into the open as the last thug falls. She looks around. The Wheeled Warrior has vanished.

DETECTIVE
What the hell...?

TRAILER VOICEOVER
Wheeled Warrior. Coming up next.

The next commercial is for the **Shea Butter & Comic Convention (SheaCon)** featuring a colorful character named **O-SHEA** enthusiastically promoting the convention while various pictures and graphics illustrate his words.

O-SHEA
It's me, O-SHEA, and it's that time again!
Get ready for the Shea Butter and Comic Convention!
Guest appearances! Artists! Vendors! Cosplay contest,
and don't forget the SHEA BUTTERRRR!
Raw shea butter! Whipped shea butter! Chunky shea butter!
Funky shea butter! Musical Guests, and
a special appearance by the Twerk-A-Gram Crew!
Moisturize yo' self! At SheaCon!

MALIK
I wish somebody would send me a Twerk-A-Gram.

HEARTLY
No, you don't.

MALIK
Uh, yeah! You a hater, for real. You can't even fathom the
beauty of a Twerk-A-Gram!

HEARTLY
Full disclosure?

MALIK
(brow furrowed, turning down the volume)
Go on.

HEARTLY
I used to work for them.

MALIK
As what, a receptionist?

Heartly just stares at him.

MALIK (cont'd)
YOOOOO!!! YOU SERIOUS?!

Malik doubles over with laughter.

MALIK (cont'd)
What in the entire hell, man?

HEARTLY
Remember that time you asked me how I, of all people,
would date the Leotep?

Malik shudders in mock horror.

MALIK
Oh noooo...

HEARTLY
Where's your drink?

MALIK
I'm... not drinking right now...

HEARTLY
(*frowning*)
Okayyyy...well I'mma tell you about this,
then you're gonna tell me about that.

MALIK
Just start talking, please.

CUT TO:

FLASHBACK:
INT. FITNESS STUDIO - AFTERNOON

Heartly is wiping sweat after a twerking class in a fitness studio with poles installed. All genders are represented in this class, even some dressed for burlesque including a few muscular, masculine guys, reminiscent of Jheri Curl's class from *Hollywood Shuffle*.

HEARTLY (V.O.)
It started when I took this fitness class - pole dancing, twerk-aerobics, burlesque, all that.

TWERK TEACHER
Great class today! Newbieeeees, don't forget your homework!

CLASS MEMBERS
(in unison)
Spread love - (class claps once in unison) - through twerk!

TWERK TEACHER
And, as promised, *(picks up a stack of fliers)* information on our new business venture!
Twerk-A-Gram has been born!

The Twerk Teacher waves the fliers as the class applauds and cheers.

TWERK TEACHER
Take a flyer! We pay WELL.

Six or seven members file past the Twerk Teacher, each taking a flyer, including a big muscular dude in a belly dance skirt with coins. Heartly is the last in line, taking a flyer and studying it.

FADE TO:

EXT. ROWHOUSE - DAY

Heartly makes her way up the front stairs of a townhouse. She's wearing a long trench coat buttoned most of the way up to the top.

HEARTLY (V.O.)
Turns out, the twerk-a-grams ain't all
birthdays and anniversaries.

A man opens the door to the townhouse.

HEARTLY
Kevin?

KEVIN
Yeah. Who are y--

Before he can fully ask his question, Heartly hits a button on her phone. "PULL YA GUNZ OUT" by Big Tony a.k.a Miss Tony plays as she sheds her trench coat and starts to twerk and rap.

HEARTLY
SHE-LEFT-YOU-FOR-YOUR-FA-THER.
IT'S O-VAH-DON'T-BOTHER...

We can only see Heartly's head and shoulders, as to only imagine how horrible her twerking skills are.

A woman walking by smoking a cigarette and walking a dog stops to stare at her.

KEVIN
You off-beat.

CUT TO:

INT. OFFICE BUILDING - DAY

The elevator doors open and Heartly gets off - again dressed in the same trench coat - and walks up to the receptionist's desk.

HEARTLY (V.O.)
And their idea of good news? It's different.

Heartly reaches the desk, hits play, drops the coat, and starts to twerk and rap to the "PULL YA GUNZ OUT" beat in the same manner:

HEARTLY
The-test-came-back-neg-a-tive.
Your-rash-should-be-gone-soon...

The woman looks embarrassed and yet, slightly relieved.

CUT TO:

INT. APARTMENT BUILDING - EVENING

Heartly makes her way up the stairs in a garden style apartment building.

HEARTLY (V.O.)
I never did get good at matching my twerks
with the messages.

Heartly knocks on a door. A massive amount of smoke emanates into the hallway as The Honorable Doctor Kimet Robinson (THDKR) opens the door.

Before he can even speak, Heartly hits play and drops the coat. The "PULL YA GUNZ OUT" beat once again blasts.

HEARTLY
Don't-come-to-work-tomorrow.
You're-fired-please-don't-sorrow...

THDKR
You not even on beat.
(*a pause as he realizes what she said*)
Wait, I'm fired? With a Twerk-A-Gram?
What kind of bullshi--

CUT BACK TO:

PRESENT DAY - HEARTLY'S LIVING ROOM

Heartly dips a chip in guacamole as Malik laughs hysterically.

HEARTLY
It was a hard day's work! I wasn't ready.

MALIK
That was all the same day??

HEARTLY
Hell yeah! I was making my money!
But, I just couldn't hack it.
And you know me, I do NOT admit defeat.
By the end of the day, I was in a bad place.

She takes a bite, making a loud crunching sound.

CUT BACK TO:

INT. APARTMENT BUILDING - EVENING

THDKR smiles at Heartly, who just finished her Twerk-A-Gram.

THDKR
QUEEN. Why dishonor yourself and degrade your ancestors
with this sad and pathetic excuse for work?
You are above this. Rise to be the Nubian Queen I see you as.
Come in. Smoke and commune with us.

Heartly is exhausted enough to take him up on it and
enters the apartment with him.

CUT BACK TO:

PRESENT DAY - HEARTLY'S LIVING ROOM

Heartly bites into another chip.

MALIK
Awwwww mannnn... he gotchu wit da Hotep smoke!

HEARTLY
(shrugs)
He got me in the right place at the right time.

MALIK
You mean the WRONG place and time! Damn!

HEARTLY
And THAT is why I don't smoke.

MALIK
Hold up.
You did that WHILE working for the city government?

HEARTLY
That's confidential. Anyway, how's your sex life?

MALIK
(stares blankly)
Why are you like this?

HEARTLY
You have something to tell me, sir.
Why aren't you drinking?

MALIK
Well, an embarrassment for an embarrassment, I suppose.
I did have a date. With a Notofearth.

HEARTLY
OH SHIT.

She grabs her wine glass and sits Indian style on the couch at rapt attention.

MALIK
(takes a deep, dramatic breath)
I met her at Miss Niecey's Romp and Stomp...

HEARTLY
Of COURSE you did.

CUT TO:

FLASHBACK:
INT. MISS NIECEY'S MERCURY RETROGRADE ROMP &
STOMP - NIGHT

The party is in full swing, everyone is having a blast. An upbeat song plays.

MALIK (V.O.)
This woman was like a dream.
Beginning to end, I--I don't know that any of this actually happened except...

Never mind, I'm getting ahead of myself.

Everything switches to slow motion as Malik sees
SAGITTARIUS at the bar. She is tall and beautiful, dark-skinned with long hair and a bangin' body.

The opening notes to an instrumental of Juvenile's "SLOW
MOTION" plays as Malik approaches her.

MALIK (V.O.)
She was sittin' at the bar,
lookin' like the baddest chick in the place...

A faint spotlight is on Sagittarius, who is wearing a
Sagittarius ribbon. There are several Sagittarius-tagged
people around her, as though they're in their own clique.

As the song continues, the scene plays like a fantasy of how
he sees her:

Sagittarius is in the center, nearly glowing, her hair blowing
magically in some imaginary wind.
The other Sagittarians are turned toward her but are
looking at Malik (the camera's view), and are doing a slow
body roll to the music.

The slow motion sequence lasts long enough for us to hear
the song's lyric, "Unnnnhh...I like it like that..."

The scene stops abruptly.

CUT BACK TO:

PRESENT DAY - HEARTLY'S LIVING ROOM

HEARTLY
WHO CARES?! What HAPPENED???

INT. CASINO - NIGHT

The Casino is abuzz with activity and excitement as people are winning and losing. An eventful night is unfolding.

MALIK (V.O.)
We made a date to meet at the casino.

HEARTLY (V.O.)
That's just tacky.

MALIK (V.O.)
Says YOU, Bougie McBoujerson.

HEARTLY (V.O.)
I'm getting bored already.

The scene suddenly fast forwards through what would have been a cool, continous shot of the casino, and starts at normal speed again with Malik and Sagittarius at the roulette table, drinking and winning. She has won an obscene amount of money/chips and a crowd has gathered.

Malik is having the time of his life.

MALIK
This is amazing! I've never seen anyone win like this.
How are you this... lucky?

SAGITTARIUS
Keep playing your cards right, and you might get lucky too.

Malik smiles broadly as we--

CUT TO:

INT. HOTEL ROOM - LATER
Sagittarius uses her hotel room key to open the door, and Malik follows her inside. She lays her purse on the dresser.

SAGITTARIUS
Sit down.

Malik does as he's told, sitting on the edge of the bed. This is clearly a first for him, and he looks a bit sheepish and vulnerable.

SAGITTARIUS
Are you scared?

MALIK
No. I'm not scared.

Sagittarius smiles at him as though she doesn't believe him.

MALIK
Question. How does the Zodiac thing work, I mean, where you're from? Notofearths have the same signs we do?

SAGITTARIUS
(shrugs with a half scoff, half laugh)
I just picked up a sash.
Do you really believe in that stuff? The Zodiac?

As the sensual, sedutive hip hop song "INCUBUS" by Dimensions plays, Sagittarius unbuttons the first button of her blouse, revealing a bit of cleavage, and stares at him with a slight smile that would otherwise be creepy if she wasn't unbuttoning her blouse seductively.

SAGITTARIUS
Let's play a game.

She pulls a large wad of cash from her bra.
She slowly and deliberately flips through the bills as though she's counting.

Malik is fascinated. Cash or cleavage? Yes.

SAGITTARIUS
I have cash stashed... everywhere.

She unbuttons another button, leans forward and waits a beat.

SAGITTARIUS
You wanna help me find it?

The camera slowly closes in on Malik's face, clearly in shock and awe.

We see rapid cuts, sensuous closeups of unmistakable skin-to-skin contact, but no clear picture of what is happening.

Intercut are quick shots of camera flashes from a phone held by the Sagittarius (we can see her baddie nail designs)

The music fades as we--

FADE TO:

INT. HOTEL - NEXT MORNING

Malik wakes up groggily. He brushes his hand over his face and $100 bills fall off of him. He sits up and more money falls off his body. He's under the sheet (presumably naked), covered in cash, and she is gone.

CUT BACK TO:

PRESENT DAY - HEARTLY'S LIVING ROOM
Heartly stares at Malik in disbelief.

HEARTLY
What?!

MALIK
I ain't finished. The next day…

CUT TO:

INT. DOCTOR'S OFFICE - DAY

Malik sits in the examination room on the raised table. He eyes the posters on the wall, diagrams, health messages about men's health, including one of the male reproductive system. A sign reads "So You Had Sex With an Alien."

His phone dings - a series of texts from an unknown number appear in succession. He opens the texts to see a series of photos of him from last night.

We hear the "Oh"s from Ludacris's "SPLASH WATERFALLS" as he begins to swipe through the pics. We don't see nudity in the photos, but can tell that each image is a bit more risqué and ridiculous than the last, each image punctuated with an "Oh!"

CUT BACK TO:

PRESENT DAY - HEARTLY'S LIVING ROOM

Heartly laughs hysterically as she snatches his phone.

HEARTLY
How you gon' start the story like Biggie *(does a Notorious B.I.G. voice impression)* "It was all a dream!" and the whole

HEARTLY (cont'd)
time you had pics of what happened?
Unlock this and lemme see!

MALIK
Oh, you wanna see me naked now?

HEARTLY
Ew. Never mind.

She tosses his phone back at him.

MALIK
Anyway, I don't remember it like it was real.

HEARTLY
(laughing)
You don't have to! That's what pictures are for! Evidence!

Malik pockets his phone.

MALIK
And anyway, I don't drink right now.

HEARTLY
(concluding her laughter)
That's smart. I think that's smart.

On the TV we see the "Wheeled Warrior" movie is starting, with the onscreen bar indicating that the volume is increasing.

INT. HEARTLY'S APARTMENT - NEXT MORNING

Heartly pours coffee from a French press into two mugs on the coffe table. Malik sits on the couch among blankets - he

120

clearly crashed on the couch last night - reading the back of the book, *The Oort Cloud* by Marvin Dixon. In his other hand is a cold slice of last night's pizza.

MALIK
Whatchu know about this?

Heartly sits down and takes the book.

HEARTLY
Don't get pizza sauce on my book!

MALIK
Uh oh.

HEARTLY
Uh oh what?

MALIK
You tryna go? Out There with THEM?

HEARTLY
And what if I was?

MALIK
You wouldn't go.

HEARTLY
Yes, I would.

MALIK
For what?

HEARTLY
Because I want to!

MALIK
You want to? You don't know what you want!
Now you think you wanna go Out There.
You think you want to date but you keep shooting everyone
and everything down--

HEARTLY
Hold on, I'm tired of everyone telling me I don't know
what I want!! You don't know me!!

MALIK
Oh, I don't?

HEARTLY
Do you know YOURSELF?
Three of YOUR last four dates ended with
you on camera being humiliated by
whatever random Black Barbie you found...

Malik is insulted but shakes off the accusation.

MALIK
Random? I don't do random.

HEARTLY
Oh, you DO do random!

MALIK
YOU the one who boned some random ass dude
you met for work on the first date!
Did you run this alien escape plan shit down to him?
Is THAT why he never called you back
after the one night stand?

HEARTLY
(gets up from the table in a huff)
I didn't call HIM back! Get that straight!

MALIK
Oh, I see.
So the one person you met that you didn't need Miss Niecey
for, you just threw away.

HEARTLY
NEED Miss Niecey?
THREW AW--you did the same damn thing I did!

MALIK
ON A DARE!

HEARTLY
Who would DO that if they weren't looking for something?
There is a hole where your soul should be!

Malik jumps up and points at her accusingly.

MALIK
A-HA!!

HEARTLY
A-HA-HELL.
I'm not the one who had to stop drinking
because I make bad decisions.

MALIK
No, you just have to leave the planet
because you make bad decisions.

Heartly's face changes from anger to hurt as she absorbs
what Malik said.

HEARTLY
And nobody wants me, right?

Heartly heads toward the bedroom.

HEARTLY (cont'd)
I'm getting the hell off this planet.
And YOU can get the hell out my house.

She storms off.

MALIK
(frustrated growl) RRRRRGGGHHHH.

Malik goes to the kitchen, grabs his blender from the counter and angrily wraps the cord around it. He grabs his coat as he storms out the apartment.

CUT TO:

INT. SENIOR LIVING FACILITY - POPS' SMALL LIVING ROOM - DAY

Malik sits in a chair at a table opposite Pops, who looks confused.

POPS
Zodiac what now?

Malik hangs his head in shame, not making eye contact.

POPS (cont'd)
Never mind. Don't bother explaining.

MALIK
I have to!

POPS
Whatchu gon' say? You was lookin' for love?
(channels Eddie Murphy's Buh-Weet)
Wookin' pa nub in aww da wong paces...

Malik is not amused.

POPS (cont'd)
You ain't a whole minute past Tig Ol' Bitty Brenda!
But here you go, usin' a datin' service?

Malik shakes his head in shame.

POPS (cont'd)
So you dig this way of life, then?
Just collectin' women like baseball cards?
Without even tryin' to live, and love?

MALIK
Pop, these women out here--

POPS
Don't give me that.
(concerned)
You got hurt. You s'posed to be the only person on Earth that
get to chase big butts and smiles but never get hurt?

Malik puts his head in his hands, defeated.

POPS (cont'd)
Chill out, son. Be good to yourself for awhile.
Give the ladies a break until you fix yourself. You broken.
They'll be there when you ready.

MALIK
(scoffs)
Unless they goin' Out There with the aliens.

POPS
(makes a face)
If they tryna do that, they already gone.

Pops taps his temple knowingly.

MALIK
Pop, suppose--

Pops cuts him off.

POPS
Let's not talk about that alien shit.
I'll cheer you up. Let's go to the mall.

MALIK
The MALL? That's new.

Pop stands and starts toward the door.

POPS
Can my girlfriend go too?

Malik stands, astounded.

MALIK
Girlfriend?!

POPS
Look, I know you been worried about me, but I'm fine here.
Got me a little lady live down the hall, got plenty to do.
I'm chillin'. And I want you to chill too.
Besides, my girlfriend? She got that Shoppin' Booty Balance.

MALIK
(softens, amused)
Aw, Pop, not you too.

Malik puts his hand on Pop's shoulder. Before it touches, a
spark jumps from his fingers.

POPS
Ow! You shocked me!

MALIK
(laughs nervously)
My bad! That was a big one!

They walk out.

FADE OUT:

FADE IN:

INT. TEA AND SAMMICHES CAFE - DAY

Heartly walks into the cafe to find a much larger crowd than usual. She makes her way through the crowd, looking confused about what's happening, until she sees a poster on an easel with Malik's picture.

It's a birthday party for "Master Malik."

HEARTLY
(sucks her teeth)
Shit.

She turns to leave but Jonathan sidles up to her dressed in his best finery.

JONATHAN
Miss Heartly!! I'm so glad you came!

HEARTLY
Uh, not really.
(looks around nervously)
I was stopping by to say hi, but I'll come back tomorrow.

JONATHAN
You're not staying?
Did you know he's announcing a book release?

HEARTLY
(with fake smile and over the top sweetness)
Wow. So many surprises.
Look, I gotta run. I'll check back again soon.

She turns away from Jonathan, starts to maneuver through the crowd and crashes right into Michael.

They look pained to see each other.

MICHAEL
Uh, hey.

HEARTLY
Heyyyyy.

She looks around nervously as Michael grabs a nearby person to diffuse the situation and pulls him in. It's Malik.

MICHAEL
Have you met my brother, Malik?

Malik's face drops when he sees Heartly.

HEARTLY
BROTHER?

She looks at Malik as if she's been stabbed in the back and storms out.

The brothers look at each other, confused. They speak at the same time.

INT. HEARTLY'S WORK CUBICLE - DAY

Heartly looks over paper documents but keeps nodding off. Her phone sitting in front of her on the desk vibrates, then makes an unusual "alien" noise that jerks her out of her sleep.

She looks at it, and a hologram projection rises out of it that reads, "Go see Miss Niecey." Heartly is shocked by the imagery she's seeing - she didn't think her phone could do that! She reaches out with a finger and pokes it through the light. The light retracts back into the phone. She draws her whole body back.

Heartly raises her head above the height of her cubicle and looks around quickly.

We see Stacey at her cubicle on the phone.

HEARTLY
(trying to get Stacey's attention)
PSSST. PSSSSSST!!

Everyone in the surrounding cubicles looks at Heartly. The cubicles are not nearly as private as we previously thought.

Stacey continues her phone call, oblivious.

Everyone is still staring at Heartly as she sits back down.

She stares at her phone, afraid to even touch it again.

MALE COWORKER (O.S.)
Ay yo, Stay-CEE, Heartly want'chu.

Heartly's phone lights up with a call, but it's on silent. Heartly stares at it, afraid to touch it. Once it stops ringing, Heartly reaches toward it nervously.

STACEY
(appears at Heartly's cubicle)
I just called you. What?

Heartly startles out of her phone trance and clutches her chest.

STACEY
What, girl?

HEARTLY
(keeping her voice low)
Lunch. Now.

STACEY
It's 9:30.

CUT TO:

INT. TEA AND SAMMICHES CAFE - MOMENTS LATER

The Cafe is empty except for Jonathan behind the counter. Heartly and Stacey sit at a small table with their coffees.

STACEY
You think that's what it's about?

HEARTLY
I have this feeling. Like I know what it's about.

STACEY
Are you scared? You know you don't have to do this.
Wait, are they gonna come looking for you or something?

HEARTLY
(unsure) No?
Well, it feels like they just did.

STACEY
Well, you can say no.
There's a lot of people trying to go.
They don't NEED you or anything.

HEARTLY
Or do they?

STACEY
Romans, Chapter 12, verse 3.
Don't think too much of yourself.

HEARTLY
(offended)
Thessalonians 4:11, mind ya business.

STACEY
Oh, so I can go back to work now?

HEARTLY
I'm sorry. I'm stressed. I haven't been sleeping well.

Heartly shifts in her seat and sips coffee. She looks out the
window at passersby. People on the street stop to look up
and point at something flying overhead.

HEARTLY
Listen. I made my decision. I'm getting out of here.
I'm done with this place.

STACEY
Heartly, are you thinking about suicide?!

HEARTLY
No! Good grief!
I'm talking about seeing what's Out There.
I know Miss Niecey can help me.

STACEY
Oh Lord, Heartly, we don't know enough.
Did you hear, a bunch of Morgan State students went
Out There? Parents don't know where they at?

HEARTLY
That's an internet rumor.

STACEY
If these people, things, whatever, can just disappear and
reappear, then they can sure make up a story about
some imaginary world.

HEARTLY
Well, now's my chance to find out.

Stacey just looks at her as if she can't believe she is really
going.

HEARTLY (cont'd)
You have your family. And a good life.

STACEY
YOU are my family.

HEARTLY
You know what I mean.

Stacey falls back into her seat. More people pass by the

window, one stops to take a picture of something above them.

HEARTLY
Stacey, don't worry about me.
Where's your faith?
What? God ain't God out there?

Stacey slowly rubs her temples.

STACEY
How am I supposed to look out for you
if you just up and leave like that?

HEARTLY
I'm not leaving YOU, I'm just...

STACEY
(sadly) Trying to go away where I may never see you again.
Got it.

Heartly takes her hand and holds it.

HEARTLY
I'm sorry. I have to do this. For me.
(trying to get Stacey to smile)
I know you won't stop praying for me.

STACEY
I'm praying for you, alright. Always.

HEARTLY
I know, and I need it. And I love you too.

Jonathan sidles up to the table unnoticed and squats down.

JONATHAN
Guess who's working the Shea Butter and
Comic Convention?!

Jonathan smiles from ear to ear as he holds up a lanyard
around his neck that reads "SheaCon."

INT. MICHAEL'S ROOM/HEARTLY'S APARTMENT - LATE
NIGHT

Michael is restless in his bed, wide awake and pondering.
Con Funk Shun's "LOVE'S TRAIN" plays as Michael appears
to perform the actions described in the song:

"Warm night, can't sleep" - Michael turns over on his back
and stares up at the ceiling;

"Too hurt, too weak, gotta call her up" - Michael grabs his
phone from the nightstand and starts to text Heartly;

"Dial that number, no one answers til two o'clock" - Michael
mans up and calls instead;

"And if by chance, you let me come over" - Heartly is
awake in her apartment watching TV. She sees the call come
up on her phone;

"Out on the street, I wanna see ya baby" - Heartly opens
the door to her apartment and stares at Michael;

"And if by chance, you let me just hold ya" - Michael and
Heartly sit on opposite ends of her sofa shyly talking and
laughing;

"I'm down on my knees, I wanna please ya baby" - Fade

into their hands reaching for each other across the back of the sofa;

"I'll be your righteous lover" - they smile at each other;

CUT TO:

INT. HEARTLY'S BEDROOM - SECONDS LATER - SONG CONTINUES

"She said Sugar" - he pulls her in and kisses her passionately;

"Honey" - close up of her shirt going over her head;

"Darlin" - close up of her back and his hands unhooking her bra;

"I really wanna see you too" - she removes his shirt then kisses him;

"It's just that someone's" - they are under the comforter, only shown from the shoulders up, then they roll over and he's on top;

"Over," - her face shows ecstasy;

"and baby" - his face shows serious love;

"I really wanna be witchu" - shot moves from them out the window into the night sky, with extra twinkly stars;

"But if by chance, you let me just hold ya" - night becomes day, camera pans back into the bedroom with Heartly and Michael lying in bed, facing each other.

Music lowers as Heartly speaks.

HEARTLY
I need you to listen to me. This is important.

The music volume picks up again.

"When in need, you said you would be here" - Michael props himself up on his elbow to listen as we-

FADE TO:

INT. SHEA BUTTER AND COMIC CONVENTION - DAY

A large hall sprawls with hundreds of people milling about, almost all in costume. As we pass through the convention we see various sights:
- A shot of the URBAN 30 SUPERHEROES in front of a step and repeat with photographers and people shouting their names.
- A shot of O-SHEA being driven through the con floor on a chariot shouting his catchphrase "Moisturize yo'self!"
- A long shot of the Twerk-A-Gram booth with people handing out flyers.

CUT TO:

INT. CONVENTION PANEL DISCUSSION ROOM - SIMULTANEOUS

Malik and two others - **PANELIST #1** (woman, Black, 30s) and **DARIUS** (a major software developer for the company Nappy Nerds wearing a full VR headset but still able to see everything that's happening) - are on the stage seated behind a table with the SheaCon logo on the table cover.

MALIK
--would do more for families of incarcerated people, as we
push to stop this abusive system that just takes more and
more of their money. We the people CAN use this technology
for our benefit, to improve our own communities.

The audience applauds respectfully.
Darius nods approvingly.

MODERATOR
Next question, please.

AUDIENCE MEMBER #1 approaches the mic, dressed
like Dave Chappelle-dressed-like-Rick James.

AUDIENCE MEMBER #1
(unexpectedly nerdy voice)
Have you guys talked to the Notofearths about,
like, their technology, and, like, how it can be used to
make games... like, better?

PANELIST #1
Better how?

AUDIENCE MEMBER #1
Like, I don't know, what do they have?
Like, they won't discuss weapons?
So like, maybe they'll discuss video games?
Do you KNOW any Notofearths, like--

PANELIST #1
You wouldn't be here if WE didn't make great games.
Not everything has to be improved by Notofearths.
We're doing just FINE.

AUDIENCE MEMBER #1
(incredulous) The world is like, going up in flames,
but everything's FINE?

MODERATOR
Security.

The audience gets restless. Security approaches Audience
Member #1 but he backs off and returns to his seat.

MALIK
(speaking over the restless audience)
Hold on. We are here to answer questions.
Let's not go unchallenged here. We can handle it.

MODERATOR
Next question.

AUDIENCE MEMBER #2 - dressed as Michael Jackson
in the "Remember the Time" video - stands up at her seat
and shouts instead of approaching the mic.

AUDIENCE MEMBER #2
ARE Y'ALL GONNA LEAVE US TO
GO OUT THERE WITH THEM?

MODERATOR
(exasperated)
Please, use the microphone.

Audience murmuring increases.

AUDIENCE MEMBER #3 grabs the mic. He is dressed
like Eddie Murray of the Baltimore Orioles, circa 1985.

AUDIENCE MEMBER #3
They say Notofearths are taking our best minds and inviting

them to go Out There. My question is, being some of our best minds, would y'all go out there and help them? Being that they've done NOTHING to help us humans?

AUDIENCE MEMBER #2
(shouting out)
That's what I just asked!!

AUDIENCE MEMBER #3
(shouting back)
WELL WE ALL WANNA KNOW!

The audience gets rowdy.
Malik raises his hands to calm the crowd.
They listen, mostly.

MALIK
Look, we have no evidence to suggest that they need our help with anything. And as far as them not helping us...
Well, that's not actually fair at all, given the fact that some very talented, intelligent, well-known people have revealed themselves to be not of Earth.
We can't just dismiss all of their contributions.

Malik pauses, seeing that the audience is now completely paying attention. Darius nods again in agreement.

MALIK (cont'd)
When we still believed them to be Earthlings, we were talking nonstop about how great they were. Now everyone just focuses on the fact that they aren't from here.

AUDIENCE MEMBER #3
You never answered the question. Are. You. Goin'?

DARIUS
First of all, they'd have to be invited.

The audience stops and all eyes are on Darius.

MODERATOR
Wait, "they"?
Are you...?

DARIUS
Yes.

The audience murmurs loudly.

MALIK
Chill! That's what I was just talking about.
Watch this. Who else here is not of Earth?

Three seconds pass. Twenty or so people raise their hands
in the audience. One second later, Audience Member #2
raises her hand. Several people in the audience voice their
frustration with an audible "AWWW!"

DARIUS
Some of y'all lyin.

A few of those with their hands up slowly lower them.

MALIK
Look at us. For the little bit of information we have,
we're letting it drive us crazy. It's nobody's business
if an individual wants to see what's Out There.
Can you imagine how brave you'd have to be
to take that leap?
To imagine leaving Earth to live your best life?

He pauses, looks out at the now silent crowd. Darius nods
his approval.

MALIK (cont'd)

I lost a dear friend because I didn't understand that.
I couldn't just let her be great. On her own terms.
And I regret it, deeply. She may leave and I'll never get to tell
her how much I respect her. This is serious, y'all.

The audience seems to be coming around to his viewpoint, some nodding in agreement.

MALIK (cont'd)

If we do know people who are going Out There,
we need to let them know how much they mean to us.
Especially if we might get to see them again.

MODERATOR

Well. Let's wrap this up.

PANELIST #1

Wait, there's one more question.

MODERATOR

Oh. Go ahead, Shadow Weaver.

Someone dressed as **SHADOW WEAVER** (from She-Ra) stands at the mic. She doesn't speak, but instead has a series of Sharpie-written poster cards.

SHADOW WEAVER (on cards)

"WHAT IS THE BEST WAY"
"TO SAY GOODBYE"
"TO A FRIEND WHO IS"
"GOING OUT THERE"

The panelists all look at each other.

MODERATOR

Anyone? Darius?

DARIUS
I got nothin'.

MALIK
I wish I knew.

Shadow Weaver removes her wig and mask to reveal she is
Heartly.

HEARTLY
(yelling with tears in her eyes)
I'LL SHOW YOU HOW! BEFORE I GO!

Malik jumps to his feet, nearly knocking over the table.

MALIK
I'm sorry, Heartly! I didn't want to lose you!

HEARTLY
I get it now! I'm sorry too!

Malik starts to make his way off the stage as Heartly starts
to head towards him. They reach each other and embrace.

They pull back to look at each other, still holding each other
by the arms.

MALIK
Movin' on, havin' fun, no tears.

HEARTLY
(crying)
Movin' on, havin' fun, no tears.

Darius nods approvingly then pops out.

Stacey and Jonathan walk up to Heartly and Malik. They

both join Heartly and Malik's hug.

AUDIENCE MEMBER #1
Worst. SheaCon. Ever.

FADE OUT.

FADE IN:

INT. - MISS NIECEY'S ASTROLOGICAL CENTRE - DAY

We hear "FOLLOW ME" by ALY-US playing at a low volume as Heartly stops in front of the dangling mobile of the solar system where she and Malik started this journey. She lets go of a large suitcase beside her and reaches up to touch a star.

As she does, Miss Niecey joins her.

MISS NIECEY
You're ready.

HEARTLY
I am ready.

MISS NIECEY
(smiling)
You can leave your baggage here.

Heartly takes a deep breath and looks around.

MISS NIECEY
I know.
Let's go.

The music volume increases as they make their way toward

143

the back of the store. The wall opens to reveal a bright light.

Miss Niecey and Heartly walk into it. There is an audible POP sound.

FADE TO BLACK.

THE CREDITS BEGIN TO ROLL AND ARE INTERRUPTED BY -

INT. MALIK'S DOCTOR'S OFFICE - DAY

Malik sits nervously on the examination table. He looks around at the posters and his eyes settle on one that reads, "Use protection. ALWAYS."

He shivers as the **DOCTOR** (male, Black, 50s) enters.

The Doctor sits on a short swivel stool and scoots up to Malik.

DOCTOR
I need to ask you...in the last month...have you...
had unprotected intercourse with... a Notofearth?

Malik pauses, then sheepishly answers.

MALIK
Yes.

DOCTOR
Mmkay. We're discovering that sometimes the Notofearths
pass on certain... for lack of a better word, abilities... through
sexual intercourse. Something about their cells interacting
with our human cells...

MALIK
Yeaahh...

DOCTOR
Have you noticed you can do anything... new?

MALIK
Well...there's this.

Malik raises his hand and begins to concentrate. Sparks form between his fingers, then grow to tiny bolts of lightning.

The Doctor looks shocked.

Malik looks into the camera and smiles as we-

FADE TO BLACK.

"FOLLOW ME" BY ALY-US BEGINS AGAIN AS THE TITLE CARD READS:
THE END?

Extra Special Thanks

In January 2020, we started filming *Caught Out There* on our own, and sought the help of backers on Indiegogo that March-- right before the Pandemic shut it down. While we're still working on completing this dream, we wanted to acknowledge and give extra special thanks to those backers who supported us early on with their donations.

Denise Mahdi
Karen Morris Carroll
Rudy Ledbetter
Jerome Rogers
Billy Taylor
Jerin Scott
Alisa Simmons
Nena Brown
Amber Davis
Karim Marshall
Sarojini Schutt
Julia Robey Christian
Dexter M. Kollie
Nancy E. Rogers
Vance Rogers
Sikani Kenjyatta
Gianina Liggett
Alex Bako
Holly White
Sean Smith
Alejandro Lorenzo

Also, an extra special shout out to the actors who helped us bring scenes to life in those early days of filming:

Tasha Powell
Dee Dee Etheridge
Cole Hansberry
Lydell Hills
Sarojini Schutt

Thank you, Kato Hammond, for your musical contributions!

About the Authors

Mahdi & Brown dreamed the concept of a platon-com in 2013 as friends who wanted to see a relationship like theirs onscreen. Three years later, they started writing the movie—and planning their 2018 wedding.

Tahira Chloe Mahdi is a community psychologist, bestselling author, college professor, and media personality. Her novel *This Is Not How It Was Supposed to Go* is a sexy, explosive adventure about community and the secrets we keep.
Learn more at TahiraChloeMahdi.com.

Christopher A. Brown is a Communications Director, videographer, graphic designer, comic book creator, and freelance writer for entertainment and gaming websites.

Though they did end up together, they still have mad respect for platonic love.